SEARCH AN

Nick Ryan

A World War 3 Technothriller Action Event

Copyright © 2021 Nicholas Ryan

The right of Nicholas Ryan to be identified as the author of this work has been asserted by him in accordance with the copyright, Designs and Patents Act 1988.

This is a work of fiction. Names, characters, places, and incidents either are the product of the author's imagination or are used fictitiously. Any resemblance to actual persons, living or dead, events, or locales is entirely coincidental.

All rights reserved. No part of this publication may be reproduced, stored in or introduced into a retrieval system, or transmitted, in any form, or by any other means (electronic, mechanical, photocopying, recording or otherwise) without the prior written permission of the author. Any person who does any unauthorized act in relation to this publication may be liable to criminal prosecution and civil claims for damages.

Dedication:

This book is dedicated to the young lady who means the world to me; Ebony.

-Nick.

About the Series:
The WW3 novels are a chillingly authentic collection of action-packed combat thrillers that envision a modern war where the world's superpowers battle on land, air and sea using today's military hardware.

Each title is a 50,000-word stand-alone adventure that forms part of an ever-expanding series, with several new titles published every year.

Facebook: https://www.facebook.com/NickRyanWW3
Website: https://www.worldwar3timeline.com

Other titles in the collection:
- 'Charge to Battle'
- 'Enemy in Sight'
- 'Viper Mission'
- 'Fort Suicide'
- 'The Killing Ground'
- 'Search and Destroy'

The War at Sea: Pacific Theater

As April drew to a bloody close, the Chinese Navy began to assert its dominance across the Pacific. Through sheer weight of numbers, China's fleets encircled the South China Sea and the Taiwan Strait in a ring of steel and missiles, strangling key international shipping routes and forcing the navies of the Pacific Allies into a desperate war of containment.

The American Navy was still reeling from the attack on the USS *Ronald Reagan* aircraft carrier in the South China Sea at the end of March that had sparked the outbreak of war. Caught unprepared by China's sudden aggressive surge, the Americans marshalled their scattered fleets to launch a series of counter attacks, and the fight for control of the oceans developed into a brutal, savage struggle.

Above the waves, the battles between enemy frigates and destroyers were small ferocious engagements fought across waterways that were streaked by the smoke trails of anti-ship missiles.

In the dark silent depths, American and Chinese attack submarines stalked each other, fighting a deadly unseen war of nerves and skill.

Enclosed in the fathomless silence of the vast Pacific, the technologically advanced US submarine fleet held the advantage. The American crews were experienced, superbly trained, and went to war in the most advanced killing machines the world has ever known.

Outnumbered, and in danger of being overwhelmed, the brave men and women of America's 'silent service' fought one heroic action after another to wrest control of the oceans back from China, and to stem the tide of China's triumphant surge west.

Gradually America's underwater dominance began to take its toll on the Chinese submarines that contested the depths. But still the battle raged unabated as China surged more and more boats further into the Pacific.

The South China Sea became the focus of China's efforts, but across the Philippine Sea and into the Western Pacific

Chinese raider submarines roamed like predatory sharks, sinking Allied merchant ships and threatening to blockade the sea lanes that kept the Allied war machine in the Pacific supplied and running.

At the end of April, American Naval Command formulated its first concerted counter-blow; a plan devised to carry the war right to China's doorstep. It was a desperate Hail Mary attempt to choke off the daunting flow of steel and missiles that continued to surge into the war zone.

It was a task that the overburdened American *Los Angeles*-class and *Virginia*-class fast-attack submarines were perfectly suited to. They sailed into harm's way with their mission goal clear and concise.

Their orders were to search and destroy.

THE WESTERN PACIFIC OCEAN

Chapter 1:

"Conn, sonar. Regained contact on Sierra One-Three, Master Nine. Now bearing two-four zero." The sound from the submarine's 21MC announcing speaker seemed harshly loud in the concentrated silence.

The Commanding Officer of the *Los Angeles*-class nuclear attack submarine, USS *Oklahoma City* (SSN-723) breathed a secret sigh of relief, but checked himself out of habit before he said anything. He leaned forward and glanced at the BQQ-10 sonar repeater to confirm the report. The squiggle of green on the screen before him was so faint as to almost be an illusion.

Commander Chris Coe reached for the 21MC speaker and snatched the microphone from its cradle, then compelled his voice into a tone of casual indifference, despite the frisson of excitement he felt. It was important that the men in the control room believed he had nerves of steel. "Sonar, Captain, aye. Can you make out what Master Nine is doing? Looks like he's maneuvering."

"Conn, sonar. Contact appears to have slowed and turned hard to the right on a major course change."

Coe, a graduate of the US Naval Academy furrowed his brow in thought.

Unbidden, Executive Officer, Lieutenant Commander Richard Wickham, scratched the back of his neck and spoke across Coe's puzzlement. "It makes no sense," he blurted. "We're in the middle of the Pacific. It seems a strange place to make such a dramatic course change."

Coe flashed Wickham a stern look and his temper spiked. He disliked his officers impulsively volunteering their unsolicited comments. He forced himself to restraint, aware that a dozen pairs of eyes were upon him, and muttered civilly.

"Concur. Perhaps, XO, the Chinese skipper suspects we have contact on him."

"It has to be a possibility," Wickham admitted, chastened by his Captain's withering glare but overcome by his anxiety.

"But it would mean the Chinese boats are far better than our intel guys ever suspected."

Sierra One-Three, Master Nine, had been classified as a Chinese Type 093 *Shang*-class submarine. The book on the Chinese vessel was pretty thin even after so many weeks at war. The Americans knew the *Shang* boats were second-generation nuclear-powered attack submarines with a top submerged speed of around thirty knots and a vertical launch system capable of firing YJ-18 anti-ship and land attack cruise missiles.

USS *Oklahoma City* had been holding intermittent contact with the Chinese submarine for two hours across the Western Pacific Ocean, with the target boat's acoustic signature fading in and out, making the task a frustrating challenge for the Americans.

Coe snatched for the 21MC again. "Sonar, conn. Is Master Nine still maneuvering?"

A few feet forward of where the two men stood speaking, a crew of four sonar operators sat at their stations, supervised by a Master Chief Sonar Technician who also kept an eye on the passive broadband displays.

"Conn, sonar. No change, Captain. Sierra One-Three still bearing two-four-zero," the Master Chief replied.

Chris Coe switched the screen on his display over to passive narrow band and studied it for a full thirty seconds like a clairvoyant trying to read tea-leaves in the bottom of a cup. Richard Wickham strode across the control room to where the fire control party worked on the starboard side of the boat. Here, in a confined area packed with sophisticated electronic and computer equipment, half a dozen men dressed in their regulation blue 'poopie suits' sat at their work stations. The screens the men worked in front of were a chaotic maze of symbols and data.

"Anything?" Wickham prompted.

No one spoke.

The Captain and the XO gravitated to the two glass-topped chart tables that dominated the aft section of the cramped space.

The XO glanced at his wristwatch. "It's been ninety seconds since we reacquired the contact, sir. This course change he has made doesn't seem to be an attempt to clear his baffles. It appears that Master Nine is following some pre-planned plot."

"Agreed," Chris Coe nodded. The Chinese Type 093 had been sailing due east, bearing zero-nine-zero, when the *Oklahoma City* had lost contact seventeen minutes earlier. Now he was heading south west.

"Could the Chinese boat be patrolling a grid section?" the XO guessed.

Coe grunted. "It's one possibility." He thought for a few seconds and then made a call guided by gut instinct.

Coe had no idea yet how far away the Chinese submarine was. The enemy boat could have been one-hundred-thousand yards, or ten-thousand yards in the distance. Prudence demanded he offset the bearing. "Officer of the Deck, make your course two-seven-zero, speed sixteen, depth five-seven-five feet."

"Aye, sir. Making my course two-seven-zero, speed sixteen, depth five-seven-five feet."

The order was repeated again by the Diving Officer of the Watch, and from the forward port side of the control room the helmsman and planesman adjusted their indicators on the SCP (Ship's Control Panel) and then gently pushed their rudder and planes control yokes, positioning the fairwater planes and stern planes to correspond with the new course and depth.

When USS *Oklahoma City* was settled on its new course astern of the Type 093 submarine, Chris Coe gave his XO a tight-lipped glance. "Bring us up behind him quietly and slowly, XO. Not a sound. Understood?" There was a tone of warning and reproof in his voice.

"Aye, aye, sir," Wickham's face was stony. He stood rigid, waiting for more; anticipating some insight into Coe's intentions, but he had learned from bitter experience not to ask, so he contrived himself to stoic silence.

Coe saw the seething questions in the other man's eyes and deliberately ignored them.

"I'll be in my stateroom. Call me immediately if Master Nine changes course or alters speed."

Coe was keenly aware of his XO's scrutiny, and could see the effort of his restraint. Coe strode from the control room, the tension between the men still crackling in the stuffy air.

It would be some time before the *Oklahoma City* closed the gap on the Chinese submarine and before Coe could take any further action. He stood in the walled confines of his tiny cabin and struggled to keep control of his emotions. The submarine had been on station for six weeks; the men were exhausted and fatigued, and he was on the ragged edge, his nerves frayed. He thought back to the brief exchange with his XO and it took all of his willpower to bring his simmering discontent under control. His relationship with his Executive Officer had deteriorated quickly since first surging from Guam at the outbreak of war. It was not Wickham's fault – it was their first tour together. Wickham did not understand Coe's style of command and was struggling to adapt.

Coe had learned through bitter experience that commanding one of the most lethal killing machines in the world was a solitary, lonely task. And so he had resolved to say nothing unnecessary, to invite no discussion under any circumstances from his officers. It was a curt, abrupt style that Wickham was grappling to come to terms with.

Coe stared around the tiny space of his cabin and then shaved, regarding his own reflection with a small shock of dismay. The face that looked back was pallid with a crop of close-cut greying hair. His eyes were glassy and bloodshot, the lines of his haggard face deeply etched around his mouth. His features looked blurred and softened around the edges, as though fatigue and strain had eroded their definition. He felt a surge of exhaustion overwhelm him, so that he clutched for the small steel sink to keep his balance.

He stripped off his clothes quickly and went through to the head that he shared with the XO. He stepped into the shower, letting the hot jets of water scald his chest. Through his fatigue and sense of lonely despair he was aware of an underlying resolve that remained unbroken. He was the commander of a nuclear fast attack boat. The lives of every man and woman aboard were in his hands. Despite the dreadful burden of command, it was his and his alone to bear. He had a responsibility to them all that could not be delegated.

If not me – who? And if not now – when?

He stepped out of the shower, dried himself and dressed quickly. Still his mind was numb with fatigue. He clenched his fists and straightened his back with a heavy sigh.

It was time to go to war.

*

When Commander Coe stepped back into the confined space of the submarine's control room, the sterile air seemed charged with a sense of suppressed anticipation. He turned slowly, his eyes taking in the features of the crew hunched over their equipment. They were tense and restless with concentration.

Coe saw his own exhaustion reflected in their faces. Some were unshaven, others wore dark bruise-like smudges below their eyes. The long weeks of unrelenting tension were taking their toll physically and mentally.

He thrust the despair and fatigue aside and put calm resolve into his voice. There was duty to do.

The fog of fatigue seemed to lift and the sound of his voice in his own ears seemed crisp and clinical – just the image he wanted to portray.

"FCC, range to Master Nine?"

The reply from the Fire Control Coordinator was almost instantaneous. "Conn, sonar. Range to Master Nine is twelve thousand yards, course unchanged at two-four-zero." Coe took a quick look around the control room. There were more men at their stations. Now the boat was actively tracking the enemy submarine there was an Officer of the Deck, a Junior Officer of the Deck, a Junior Officer of the Watch and two Fire Controlmen of the Watch.

Coe grunted. Twelve thousand yards. He could fire his torpedoes right now.

"Officer of the Deck, reduce speed to eight knots, maintain depth five-seven-five feet and man battle stations torpedo." It seemed counterintuitive to slow speed, rather than increase speed to close the distance, but submarine warfare was a painstaking process. Increasing speed would diminish the *OKC*'s ability to track target changes.

"Aye, sir. Decreasing speed to eight knots, maintaining depth five-seven-five feet. Manning battle stations torpedo."

Coe turned to Richard Wickham who was in the role of Fire Control Coordinator. Wickham passed the order to the torpedo room.

"Torpedo room, fire control. Make tubes one and two ready in all respects."

The response was almost immediate. "Make tubes one and two ready in all respects. Fire control, torpedo room, aye."

Wickham blinked a trickle of sweat from his eyes. Moments later the order was completed and the torpedo room acknowledged that tubes one and two were ready for firing. Wickham passed on the information to Captain Coe, his voice reflecting the XO's own rising tension.

"Captain, tubes one and two are ready in all respects."

"Very well. Firing Point Procedures for Master Nine the *Shang*, single Mk 48 ADCAP."

Quickly the principal officers on duty gave their reports.

"Ship ready," the OOD responded.

"Solution ready," the Fire Control Coordinator said a moment later.

"Weapons ready," Weps said.

Coe closed his eyes for an instant. He had done everything right. Their stealthy approach towards the enemy boat had been textbook. They were in the Chinese boat's baffles, undetected and unexpected, yet the tactical situation gave Coe no particular satisfaction. It had been due to a measure of luck, not skill, that they had reacquired the enemy submarine. If the fortunes of war had been a little crueler *OKC* might now be seconds away from destruction…

Around Coe the BSY-1 operator and the XO were patiently checking the TMA (Target Motion Analysis) solution on Master Nine. Wickham and Coe exchanged a glance of confirmation.

The CSO (Combat Systems Officer) repeated the target submarine's speed, course and finally the range.

"Sonar, conn. Stand by," Coe snapped.

"Conn, sonar, standing by."

Throughout the *Oklahoma City* the tension ratcheted up. It was as if every man aboard collectively held their breath. Coe felt a tight fist of tension clench in the pit of his guts. He thrust out his jaw and drew his lips tight so the words when he spoke them seemed to hiss with savagery. "Shoot on generated bearings, tube one, Master Nine."

"Shoot on generated bearings, tube one, Master Nine, aye!"

A second later the *Oklahoma City* seemed to tremble with a liquid pulse of energy that sent a tremor through the entire length of the submarine.

The Mk 48 ADCAP (Advanced Capabilities) torpedo surged from its tube and dashed towards its target. The Mk 48s were fast, deep-diving and highly maneuverable – widely regarded as the most advanced torpedoes in the world. Charged with a six-hundred-and-fifty-pound warhead of PBXN-103 explosive and an electromagnetic fuse, they were nineteen-foot-long lethal killers. Each torpedo was wire-guided to allow crucial targeting data to be relayed between the weapon and the BSY-1 fire control system aboard *Oklahoma City* up until the point where the torpedo reached the terminal stage of its attack. Then the Mk 48 became autonomous; using its powerful active seeker in the nose of the weapon to detect and close on the target.

Once the torpedo was racing across the dark ocean void the Combat Systems Officer reported the weapon had launched successfully.

The Mk 48 executed its wire clearance maneuver and began to accelerate to its top speed of over fifty knots. The Sonar Supervisor relayed the information to Captain Coe. "Conn, sonar. Weapon running normally. No target alertment."

Coe acknowledged the message with a curt, "Very well," keeping his face utterly impassive. He wanted to pace the tight confines of the room but fought the urge. He had to be seen as the man of steely nerves. "Time to acquisition?"

"Five minutes, fifty-five seconds, Captain," the Fire Control Coordinator replied. Not on Chris Coe's boat would any man dare refer to him casually as 'skipper' or 'skip'. He was Captain Coe at all times, even to his highest-ranking officers.

The seconds passed with agonizing slowness and in the fraught tension every man at his station seemed gripped with tense apprehension. Coe compelled himself to nonchalant indifference, keeping his face expressionless and resisting the urge to fidget, nor make any unnecessary comment. The control room was quiet as a morgue as the torpedo continued on its inexorable course.

Finally sonar reported, the metallic voice over the 21MC jarring and abrupt across the tense silence. "Conn, sonar. Weapon slowing… weapon enabled." There was a momentary pause and then sonar reported, "Detect! Detect! Target range eleven thousand yards. Course two-four-three, speed fifteen knots."

Fire Control added, "Solution good. No updating."

The Chinese submarine became aware of its impending doom just seconds before the Mk 48 struck home. The reverberating explosions through the ocean sounded to the men aboard the *Oklahoma City* like a savage rumble of thunder that whipped and cracked around them.

"Shut the outer doors and reload tube one."

Someone in one of the boat's passageways started to cheer in triumph and the celebration was taken up by the rest of the crew. Captain Coe turned on the men in the control room and barked at them.

"Enough!" he snapped, simmering with fury. "There's nothing here to celebrate. We were lucky. We didn't out maneuver our enemy. We didn't beat them in a tactical battle. We were fortunate to chance upon their sonar signal. If fate had been different, it could be us on the receiving end of a Chinese torpedo. Remember that."

The ragged cheers were cut short. A couple of men looked sheepish and chastened. A sonar operator hung his head and shuffled uneasily on his seat. Coe continued to glare around the room, withering men with the force of his fury until a sudden barked voice slashed across the tense still air.

"Conn, sonar!" the Master Chief Sonar Technician's voice was fraught with alarm. "Torpedo in the water bearing two-seven-zero, designate Sierra One-Four," then added urgently, his voice becoming shrill. "High pitch screws! We have two torpedoes in the water! Steady bearing rates. Bearing two-seven-one and two-seven-three!"

*

"Steady course one-five-zero!" Chris Coe's reaction was intuitive. His objective was to place the enemy torpedoes on the edge of *OKC's* baffles. "All ahead flank. Make your depth eight hundred feet!" He reached for the *Oklahoma City's* 1MC system and snapped, "Rig ship for depth charge!" The 1MC was the boat's main circuit that acted as a ship-board public address system. Coe's order reached every space within the submarine instantly.

A general emergency alarm sounded and men went scrambling to their collision and damage control stations.

"Conn, sonar. Torpedoes are Yu-6s, now bearing two-eight four and two-eight seven. It's another Chinese *Shang*-class boat!"

Coe spun around and stared at the sonar monitor on the conn. He saw two bright traces and cursed bitterly. *Oklahoma City* had been bounced by a second Chinese submarine. Now the racetrack pattern the first *Shang* had been sailing made sense; the two Chinese boats had been planning a mid-ocean rendezvous.

Oklahoma City's abrupt acceleration had caused the submarine to cavitate, leaving a knuckle of violently disturbed water in the ocean. The large bubbles of collapsing steam created an enticing acoustic return to act as a lure for the approaching torpedoes. However, the two Yu-6 weapons ploughed straight through the disturbance, undeterred.

The deck beneath Coe's feet tilted dramatically as the submarine went into a high-speed dive. He shifted his weight to maintain his balance, his thoughts racing as he visualized a three-dimensional image of the tactical situation.

The game-clock in his mind started ticking. He waited for a heartbeat and then suddenly ordered, "Launch countermeasures!"

The order was repeated crisply by the XO and then the COB. A moment later two ADC Mk3 tubes were launched from their dispensers at the submarine's stern planes. The ADCs were six-inch diameter torpedo and sonar countermeasures carried aboard every American submarine. Once ejected, the ADCs hovered vertically in the ocean's depths, using a pressure-controlled motor to drive a small propeller in the tail of each decoy. They activated immediately, emitting an acoustic signal to decoy enemy torpedoes.

Bearing lines to the two Chinese torpedoes flashed across the combat control consoles. The enemy weapons were closing rapidly and about to reach the countermeasures.

Coe made the calculations and figured the first enemy torpedo would impact in three minutes. He stole a glance around the control room. The crew were frenetic, hunched at their stations, their faces rigid. Despite the frigid cold air circulating throughout the submarine, the room felt stuffy and heated. Coe saw several men steal glances in his direction, expecting a rush of barked orders. Every man in the room understood they were only moments from death.

Chris Coe smiled like a wily old fox, and then calmly gave his next order, finally free from self-doubt and exhaustion and fatigue: at last in his element. "Come left to zero-nine-zero."

The helmsman changed course, bringing the submarine around quickly. Coe ordered the submarine down to one thousand feet, his voice betraying no emotion. American torpedoes were unrivalled anywhere in the world and unaffected by depth. The torpedoes used by other nations were prone to leaking and slower speeds at great depths. By taking *OKC* deep Coe was giving himself an additional edge in the fight for survival.

The crew in the control room exchanged awed glances at the Captain's icy calm. Some wore expressions of sheer disbelief. The submarine settled on its new course and depth just as the excited voice from sonar blared from the overhead speaker.

"Conn, sonar! Explosions in the water. Both Chinese torpedoes went for the countermeasures and detonated."

Coe simply nodded, as if the announcement came as no surprise, then his eyes sought out Richard Wickham. "XO, range to Sierra One-Four?"

Wickham straightened from the glass-topped plot table at the aft of the control room. "Eleven thousand yards, Captain. Target has been re-designated as Master Ten, and is turning to the northeast, bearing zero-six-three. I have a firing solution."

Coe nodded. He needed to slow the boat to regain tactical control. "Officer of the Deck, make your speed five knots."

"Making my speed five knots, aye, sir," the OOD repeated the order with just enough strain in his voice to betray his tension.

"Make tubes one and two ready in all respects."

The order was repeated and then Coe calmly signed the Chinese submarine's death warrant. "Firing point procedures, Master Ten," Coe said.

"Ship ready!" the OOD said.

"Solution ready!" the XO said.

"Weapons ready," Weps confirmed.

"Shoot on generated bearings, tube two, Master Ten."

"Shoot on generated bearings, tube two, Master Ten, aye!"

Oklahoma City lurched as the Mk 48 torpedo erupted from its tube with a slamming whoosh of sound and turned onto an intercept course with the Chinese *Shang* once it left the *OKC*. Trailing its guidance wire, the torpedo quickly accelerated to top speed, closing inexorably on the enemy boat.

Coe waited, simmering with impatience. It was important that the boat shot at slow speed and then resisted any major course changes until the wire from the Mk 48 torpedo was deployed and working. After several thumping heartbeats he drew a deep breath and lowered his voice until it sounded like a moment of casual conversation. "All ahead two-thirds," Coe said. "Make your depth three-two-eight feet."

"Making my speed all ahead two-thirds. Making my depth three-two-eight feet, aye, sir," the COB repeated. American submarine commanders were trained to avoid even depth levels such as two hundred, or three hundred feet as a condition of good tactical practice. *Oklahoma City* began to slow and ascend, once again her deck tilting as the submarine rose from the depths.

"Conn, sonar. Torpedoes are running normal at high speed."

The American and Chinese submarines were on diverging courses. Coe wanted to put space between himself and the enemy boat.

Suddenly the Sonar Chief turned in his seat. "Master Ten has alerted. He's just accelerated. I've got a blade count; he's doing turns for twenty-three knots."

"Transients?" the XO asked impetuously. "Is he flooding his tubes?"

"Negative," the Sonar Chief clamped a hand over his headphones, frowned, then shook his head. "He's just running like hell."

Typically, a submarine Captain would react automatically to an incoming torpedo, increasing speed, abruptly changing course, and then firing a homing torpedo back along the line of bearing at his attacker. The Chinese skipper aboard the *Shang* had only self-preservation on his mind.

"Master Ten now making twenty-five knots," the Sonar Chief began a running commentary.

"Detect! Detect! Homing! Torpedo one has acquired target," the torpedo launch controller added his excited voice to the fraught tension.

"Cut the wires to torpedo one. Post launch tube one. Shut the outer doors," Chris Coe ordered quietly.

The Chinese submarine's fate was sealed. As the seconds counted down to impact, the enemy skipper tried another radical course change, leaving an effervescing knuckle of billowing bubbles in its wake, but the Mk 48s burst straight through it and reacquired their target on the far side of the disturbance. The *Shang* went into a sudden deep dive in a last desperate attempt to break the contact. When the Mk 48 reached its target and detonated, the enemy submarine was in six hundred feet of water.

The sound of the *Shang's* destruction was a brutal thunder of echoing noise.

*

Chris Coe spent sixty cautious seconds studying the sonar repeater in the forward corner of the control room before ordering *Oklahoma City* to periscope depth to collect the regularly scheduled twenty-thirty satellite downlink and to report the destruction of the two *Shang*-class Chinese submarines.

"Sonar, conn. Report all contacts."

"Conn, sonar. I have no contacts."

"Conn, aye."

The *Oklahoma City* came up from the deep in a cautious ascent, pirouetting in the water as she rose to allow her sonar to clear her baffles and check for surface ships. Going to periscope depth was fraught with danger because – despite technology's best efforts – the temperature stratification of shallow water above one hundred feet caused by the heating of the sun made the presence of thermal layers hard to hear through. Often the presence of a quiet ship went undetected by the submarine until they were in the same layer or could see visually.

As the submarine ascended, the only voice was that of the Diving Officer calling out the depths. When the submarine had risen to a depth of one hundred and fifty feet, the OOD spoke.

"Captain, the ship is at one-five-zero feet. All ahead one third making turns for four knots and on course two-four-zero. I have cleared baffles and hold no sonar contacts. Request permission to go to PD and clear the twenty-thirty hours broadcast, get a fix, and send a naval message on the engagement."

"Very well, proceed to periscope depth."

The submarine rose to a depth of sixty feet. Coe waited until the boat leveled, the periscope was raised and a safety sweep had been made. He heard the OOD make his next report.

"No close contacts."

"No threat contacts," ESM reported. "Request permission to raise the ESM mast."

"Chief of the Watch, raise the ESM mast," the OOD confirmed.

As soon as the periscope broke the surface a speaker in control started blaring the ESM environment. Coe's trained ear listened carefully for any high PRF and high signal strength radars.

The Type 18 periscope was a highly sophisticated marvel of modern technology that included a self-contained ESM receiver as well as video, IR and high-speed cameras. In high threat environments only the submarine's periscope was brought above the surface in order to limit the boat's telltale radar cross-section and visual detection vulnerability.

The periscope assistant worked the operating ring to raise the periscope, then snapped the handles into place as it came out of the well. With his stop watch around his neck he would help align the correct bearing looking back at the digital readout. Chris Coe stepped to the periscope pedestal.

"Sonar?" Coe double-checked.

"I hold no contacts."

Coe bent his right eye to the viewing lens. He duck-walked a full circle to check the horizon. Submariners called the routine 'dancing with the one-eyed lady'. There was nothing visible on the surface in hi or low power.

A radioman announced over the 21MC circuit, "All traffic aboard and accounted for."

Captain Coe reached up, placed the scope forward, brought up the handles and rotated a large orange ring clockwise. The periscope slid back into the well. "OOD, let's secure from battle stations and get back down deep."

"Aye, sir," the OOD nodded and then went on, "Secure from general quarters. Diving officer, make your depth three-two-five feet, all ahead standard. All stations, conn going deep."

"Sonar, aye."

"Radio, aye."

"ESM, aye."

The COW turned to the Captain. "Sir, all masts and antennas indicate down."

"Very well, Chief of the Watch. All stations, conn, securing the open Mic."

Several minutes later the XO appeared in the control room carrying an old fashion clipboard, despite the fact that modern technology beamed the message directly to the boat's stations.

It was one of Chris Coe's eccentricities to insist on adhering to minor naval traditions that did not affect the performance of the boat. Wickham showed the downloaded satellite message to Coe who blinked, startled, and then frowned.

"We've been recalled immediately to Guam, Captain."

Coe nodded, but remained tight-lipped, despite his shock.

What could be so important that it would necessitate a Los Angeles-class submarine to abandon its patrol in the middle of a war zone?

APRA HARBOR
GUAM

Chapter 2:

Once *Oklahoma City* surfaced west of Guam and began its approach to Apra Harbor, a buzz of electric anticipation swept through the boat. In the wardroom, the submarine's junior officers watched the periscope feed on the widescreen TV monitor while in the cockpit atop the submarine's sail, Chris Coe was a picture of stern, silent focus.

As the boat approached the channel markers and prepared to navigate Guam's problematic inner harbor, two snub-nosed Tiger-Tug tugboats bustled forward to take the submarine in tow, their moves coordinated by a harbor pilot who was in the cramped cockpit; passing advice to the bridge in the calm clear voice of a seasoned professional.

In the officer's wardroom, the view on the TV monitor was dominated by a huge rock cliff-face called Orote Point to the south and a low rock wall constructed atop a band of coral reefs to the north. Beyond the foreground, and set against the backdrop of the island's rising mass, several Military Sea Lift Command ships were at anchor in the outer harbor.

Oklahoma City moved ahead cautiously, making each channel turn crisply under the guidance of the two tugs, and gliding towards the inner harbor with a broom secured to the weather bridge. It was a tradition dating back more than seventy years to the Second World War, signifying that the submarine had carried out a 'clean sweep' of enemy targets. Coe – being old-school navy – had insisted the ritual be observed and continued now that war had once more come to the world.

The breakwater slid quietly astern, and the boat slowed then turned around a reef towards the entrance to the inner harbor. The shoreline was littered on one side with several rusting hulks anchored in front of the Guam Shipyard. Opposite stood the main American Naval Base. Coe saw a military supply ship docked at Polaris Point, and recognized it instantly as USS *Emory S. Land* (AS-39), one of the US Navy's two operating submarine tenders. The tender was moored with her stern facing towards the pier at an angle that allowed submarines to tie up on both sides of the vessel. Beyond the tender, and dwarfed by her steel bulk, Coe saw the low silhouette of an SSGN *Ohio*-class guided missile submarine. He raised his binoculars and stared at the boat. It was tied up on the *Emory S. Land's* starboard side. He shifted the focus of his attention inland.

Beyond the pier stood a cluster of small buildings and a parking lot. There were a dozen trucks parked and a small crowd of people in civilian clothes moving towards the shoreline. Coe saw two waiting cranes and a cluster of military vehicles lined in neat rows. The frown on his face deepened. The civilians would be wives, girlfriends and children of his crew, eagerly awaiting the return of loved-ones. But the knot of military vehicles puzzled him. He swept the binoculars back to the SSGN but detected no sense of activity, no bustle of movement that might suggest the boat was in the process of re-supplying or re-arming.

Coe lowered the glasses and let them hang from the strap around his neck, overcome with a sense of sudden ominous foreboding…

*

There was a car waiting at the end of the pier and a petty officer in the driver's seat. Even before Coe had climbed a rope ladder from the cockpit down to the deck, a small crane had begun lifting a brow into position, and *OKC's* in-port colors were raised; a national ensign was struck from the bridge and another ensign was hung from the stanchion on the after deck.

Richard Wickham joined Coe on the aft deck as the last of the lines were being doubled up and stood without speaking.

"I'm leaving, XO."

Without another word Coe saluted the ensign and strode across the brow onto firm land for the first time in weeks. In the background the 1MC loudspeaker announced, "*Oklahoma City* departing."

The petty officer scrambled from the car, saluted Coe, and held the passenger-side door open for him. Coe returned the salute and climbed inside the vehicle.

The drive to the Squadron Fifteen headquarters building was short and passed in a blur. Coe stepped out at the main entrance of a modern building that had been extensively refurbished in recent years to reflect the growing significance of Guam to America's influence in the Pacific. He was met at the front doors by another petty officer who escorted him through a labyrinth of corridors and narrow well-lit passageways. "The Squadron Commodore has been expecting you, sir," the young naval officer stopped suddenly in front of a closed door. "Please go right in."

The commodore's office was sparsely decorated with austere military furnishings, a couple of wilting pot plants and a bank of filing cabinets along one wall. Behind the desk a window overlooked the expanse of Apra Harbor, spilling bright daylight into the room.

Commodore Theodore S. Cinderman was a small, compact man with a frosting of short-cut grey hair and a watchful, serious face behind black-rimmed spectacles. He rose to his feet courteously and held out his hand as Chris Coe stepped into the office. "Congratulations, Coe, on a most successful mission."

"Thank you, Commodore," Coe shook hands, standing stiffly. "All credit goes to my officers and crew. They've worked hard for weeks on end and they're exhausted. But they're professionals – and good people. They're all looking forward to some rest time ashore…"

The Commodore nodded, his eyes dark. His expression hardened when Coe mentioned the exhaustion of his crew. "I'm afraid that's no longer possible, Captain Coe. I have a new set of orders requiring you to sail again in thirty-six hours," there was uncompromising finality in the Commodore's voice. "You will re-load and re-supply for an eight-week operation."

Coe's face tightened. He felt the blood drain from his face. A protest leaped to his lips but his training and discipline choked the words off. The Commodore watched Coe's silent fight to restrain himself with detached interest. In war there could be no room for compassion. The Commodore's eyes turned cold. "You'll be sailing back into harm's way."

"The mission, sir?" Coe felt himself swaying on his feet. A wave of fatigue washed over him but he crushed down on it.

"Operation Close Quarters," the Commodore reached for a thick file on his desk and handed it over. Coe took the file and left it unopened; it was irrelevant. In the modern American Navy, all orders were sent to the ships electronically. Everything contained in the folder would be on his computer when he returned to the boat. "According to HUMINT and some ELINT from our intelligence people, we believe the Chinese are planning to send a major munitions convoy from Qingdao Harbor in sixteen-days' time. That in itself is unremarkable," the Commodore clasped his hands behind his back and began to idly prowl the room as he spoke, pausing for a moment to stare out the window at the view across the harbor. "But we believe this planned convoy is special, both because of the suspected munitions being transported, and their possible destination. A source suggests that the convoy is bound for Gwadar Harbor on the Arabian Sea. Important people in Washington believe this convoy might be part of an arms shipment from China designed to tempt Pakistan into joining the war."

The Commodore turned suddenly and saw shock and then dawning understanding of the dire implications on Coe's face. The Commodore nodded, his own expression grey and grave. "That's why we need your boat, Chris," the Commodore used Coe's Christian name for the first time. "I wouldn't be handing you this task if it wasn't critical."

Coe nodded. "I understand, sir."

"Your mission is to conduct unrestricted submarine warfare against any and all Chinese targets to ensure that convoy does not leave the Yellow Sea – but you won't be alone. Once on station you will lay off Qingdao and monitor Chinese shipping movements until two *Virginia*-class submarines currently engaged on other missions complete their activities and converge to mount a coordinated attack. The other boats will sortie from Yokosuka, Japan. Once *Minnesota* and *Colorado* make the rendezvous, Captain Gainsborough, aboard *Minnesota*, will assume overall tactical command for the attack."

Coe nodded. He knew and respected Arnold Gainsborough as a wily, skilled submariner; the two men had been at USNA together. Gainsborough had been an upper classman in Coe's Company.

"I understand, sir."

The Commodore nodded, then seemed to change tack. "How are your men?"

"Tired, sir."

The Commodore nodded. "We're all tired," he conceded. "And the demands of this war are going to get a lot worse before it gets better. What is the material condition of your boat?"

"Ship-shape, sir. We have a faulty carbon dioxide scrubber, but it's nothing that can't be quickly repaired with parts from the tender."

"Nothing else requires immediate attention?"

"Nothing out of the ordinary that cannot be fixed within twenty-four hours if I direct the tender's CO to bring all of his resources to bear."

"Your XO?"

"What about him, sir?"

The Commodore paused, as though searching for a delicate way to ask an important question. "Are you an effective team?"

Coe's expression tightened. "It's a clash of cultures, Commodore. I'm old school. I've been driving boats for a long time. Lieutenant Commander Wickham is a fine officer. We have a working relationship," Coe said diplomatically.

The Commodore arched his eyebrow quizzically at the reply but let the comment hang in the air, uncontested. Instead, he switched the discussion back to Operation Close Quarters and the lead up to the mission. "When you depart Guam, you will first be escorting USS *Emory S. Land*, USNS *Robert E Peary* and USNS *Washington Chambers* west towards the Celebes Sea. Those ships are needed for operations with the 7th Fleet. Once you reach the Celebes, you'll rendezvous with USS *Alexandria* north of Karakelong Island. *Alexandria* will take over escort duties and delouse your boat before you make your speed run north to China."

"Aye, aye, sir," Coe thought quickly. The *Robert E Peary* and the *Washington Chambers* were both *Lewis and Clark*-class dry cargo replenishment ships with a top speed of maybe twenty knots. The *Emory S. Land* submarine tender was probably a couple of knots slower. It would be an excruciatingly slow transit across the western Pacific through hostile waters. "Will *Emory S. Land* be ready to sail in time, sir?"

It was a major operation to get a submarine tender underway. The ships were usually in port for long periods of time and required a lot of connections to shore in order to function.

"She'll be ready," the Commodore nodded. "She's been waiting for your return. Most of the ship's departure preparations have already been completed."

The Commodore went back behind his desk, seeming to signal the meeting was concluded. Coe hesitated, then saluted and turned on his heel. When he reached the door, the Commodore suddenly spoke again, calling across the room.

"Commander Coe? Can I give you a nickel's worth of free advice?"

Coe stopped with his hand on the doorknob and turned warily. 'Advice' from a Commodore was navy-speak for criticism. "Certainly, sir," he tried to keep the flush of temper from rising to his cheeks.

The Commodore smiled thinly and lowered his voice in an attempt to soften his words. "Trust your senior guys in the wardroom. Your Number One and Number Two are men you must learn to depend on. I said it before and I meant it; this war is going to get worse before it gets better. It's too much of a burden for any one man to handle alone, Commander. Your officers are good men, and if you're holding the reins too tightly, you're going to strangle the life out of a fluid command structure that has worked successfully for seven decades of undersea warfare… and in the process, you might just put your boat and your crew's lives at risk."

*

When Chris Coe returned to the submarine from his briefing at Squadron Fifteen headquarters, the pier was already crammed with forklifts, cranes and pallets of dehydrated food stores. *Oklahoma City's* topside was tangled with gear and her weapons-loading hatch forward of the sail was open. The boat's Weapons Officer and the Chief of the Boat were supervising a gang of ten dockworkers as they prepared to begin the delicate task of replenishing the boat's store of Mk 48 torpedoes. Each man wore a colored hardhat, and several were dressed in hi-viz colored vests.

Down inside the submarine, the second deck's flooring had been removed and then carefully reassembled to form a makeshift loading frame that reached down from the topside weapons hatch all the way to the torpedo room situated on the third deck where a transport frame waited to move the torpedoes to their final positions within the torpedo room.

"*Oklahoma City* returning," the 1MC barked to announce that the Captain was back on board.

Richard Wickham appeared through a hatch and made his report, striding across the thick rubber acoustic tiles that enveloped *Oklahoma City's* hull. He was wearing blue coveralls and a brown, high-collared 'submarine' sweater, despite the warm afternoon weather. He caught up with Coe by the Forward Escape Trunk.

Coe ran his eyes across the deck. There was a sense of bustling energy about everything being done, and despite the apparent chaotic frenzy of movement and noise, he could see that work was proceeding with order and efficiency. He glanced to the pier where the cranes that slung the Mk 48 torpedoes were carefully moving into position and grunted. "You seem to have everything in hand, XO. I assume the men have heard the news that we're shipping out again in thirty-six hours."

"Yes, sir. We got word," Wickham said.

"How are the crew?"

"They're not happy, sir," Wickham admitted. "They've been at sea for a long time and they were looking forward to being reunited with family. But they know there's a war on, and they know their duty. They believe the mission we've been given must be important."

Coe nodded. "It is. Meet me in my cabin in two minutes time."

Coe dropped down through the open hatch into the athwart ship's passageway – the demarcation line between the forward end of *OKC* and engineering. He went forward, through the crew's mess and then up a short ladder to the navigation space, then into the control room, past the conn and ship's control station to his stateroom.

The passageways were crammed with crewmen moving purposely throughout the lower decks and with work crews who were clearing space for the food stores that the submarine would need to carry when she departed. The corridors were so narrow that when two men passed each other, they had to turn sideways, their chests brushing together briefly. The faint chemical aroma that tainted the chilled air aboard the submarine struck Coe immediately. It was a part of submarine life; an ammonia-type odor that permeated everything aboard the boat, made even starker by the comparison to the warm sweet air he had been breathing topside.

The Captain's stateroom was little larger than a public phone booth, paneled with wood-grained Formica. Not an inch of the available space was wasted. The settee folded down into a bunk, and even the Captain's desk against the after bulkhead folded away when not needed. Below the desk were drawers, and in the wall above hung a safe that contained some of the ship's most classified documents. To the left of the safe stood a bank of electronic panels and a telephone handset connected to critical locations throughout the boat.

Chris Coe sat down at the desk. Richard Wickham appeared in the open doorway, his expression expectant.

The Captain quickly scanned the message boards that were waiting for him, then rubbed his chin. The stubble along the line of his jaw crackled under his fingers. He thought pensively for a long moment then, with effort of will and the Commodore's advice still echoing in his ears, he beckoned his XO in. "Shut the door behind you."

Wickham closed the door and sat in the small space, frowning. Beyond them the sounds of *OKC* preparing to get underway ebbed and flowed. Coe kept his voice low and gave Wickham a thumbnail sketch of their orders and then warned, "But I don't want anyone else aboard to know the details of our mission until we're submerged and at sea. We'll brief the wardroom only after we are well clear of Guam. Understand?"

Wickham nodded, his mind already wrestling with the challenges ahead. "What about the pre-underway briefing?"

"You and the Nav can brief the underway," Coe said. "Let's keep everything as normal as possible until we clear Apra Harbor."

"Aye, sir."

"Our first challenge is to get the supply ships and the tender safely to the Celebes Sea. We're going to have to be at our best for that to happen. I've no doubt the Chinese have more *Shangs* lurking in the western Pacific and we're going to be tethered to escort duty until we meet up with *Alexandria*. The enemy may already be aware through intelligence sources that a convoy is preparing for departure from Guam. It's certainly hard to hide the fact that we're preparing to underway and if they have a covert intel source here on the island, you can be sure they will arrange a welcoming party to intercept us."

Chapter 3:

At 2100 the following evening, *Oklahoma City* finally departed Apra Harbor without fanfare, under the cover of darkness and driving into the teeth of an approaching storm. The night was black and the wind-whipped chop across the harbor added to the challenges of the departure.

Because of the heavy weather Coe had decided on a minimal bridge rig – just the OOD, himself and a Phone talker, with the lookout remaining down inside the enclosed area of the sail and no watch-standers.

"Captain, request permission to get *Oklahoma City* underway," the Officer of the Deck said formally when everything was in readiness.

"Officer of the Deck, get the ship underway."

"Get the ship underway, aye, sir," the OOD's face was taut as he stared into the heaving, howling night. A squall of thundering rain swept over the submarine. He contacted the harbor pilot on the bridge-to-bridge radio and ordered him to stand-by. The pilot responded; his own voice tight. He was stationed aboard the tug tied to the *OKC's* bow, ready to pull the massive submarine away from the side of the pier.

"Phone talker to the forward deck, cast off all lines!" the OOD had to raise his voice to a bellow to be heard above the maniacal flute of the wind, even though the Phone talker was close beside him.

"Cast off all lines, aye, sir," the voice in reply from the deck sounded far away, whipped by the wind when it came back to the bridge through the speaker.

The OOD waited a heartbeat, then reached for the bridge's 7MC microphone. "Helm, bridge. Train the outboard to starboard."

"Outboard is trained to starboard, ninety."

The OOD glanced aft immediately to ensure the submarine was moving in the intended direction, then raised the pilot aboard the tug. "Prepare to pull easy on the bow."

"All lines cast off," the Chief of the Boat called again from the deck when the last of the mooring lines had been released and the submarine was free from restraint.

The *OKC* did not sound its whistle to announce its departure and the tug had been cautioned to similar silence prior to the underway.

The OOD eased the submarine away from the pier and the huge sleek steel monster slowly pirouetted until its bow was pointed down the length of the channel towards the outstretched arms of the breakwaters.

"Cast off tug," the OOD sent the instruction to the forward deck via the Phone talker and waited for the response.

"Cast off tug, aye."

The OOD repeated the order into the *OKC*'s control room. "Navigator, casting off the tug."

Down below, within the belly of the steel beast, Richard Wickham made the announcement on the 1MC. "*Oklahoma City* is underway, time twenty-one-seventeen hours." The news around the submarine was greeted with solemn silence.

Crosscurrents at the mouth of the outer harbor were notoriously difficult because the entrance was the most western point of the island, wedged between the thrust of Glass Breakwater to the north and Orote Point to the south. A mile beyond the island the ocean plunged to depths beyond six thousand feet, meaning that the ocean currents came right up to, and sweep right across, the harbor entrance. With just a thousand feet between the northern and southern breakwalls and the ever-present danger of a lurking coral reef, exiting in daylight and in calm weather proved challenging. At night, in the face of a seething storm and with a two-knot crosscurrent, it was a tense and difficult hour of concentrated work on the bridge for the OOD and Chris Coe.

*

The OOD reached up and pulled the lower bridge hatch closed, then spun the hand wheel several times. "Last man down. Hatch secured."

The acting Officer of the Deck repeated the words to confirm the hatch was secured and *Oklahoma City* prepared to dive. The Chief of the Watch ran a wary eye over a bank of warning panels to confirm that all the submarine's hull openings were indicating 'shut'. "Straight board."

Coe spun on his heel and his eyes sought out the OOD. *Oklahoma City* was wallowing in heavy swells, the deck swaying at steep angles beneath his feet and he was impatient to get below the heaving ocean's surface. "Officer of the Deck, are we ready to dive?"

Prompted by the tone of Coe's voice the OOD nodded crisply. "Captain, the ship is rigged for dive, the compensation entered, the ship is ready for dive."

"Very well," Coe had his hands clasped gripped behind his back, balancing on the balls of his feet. "Very well. Submerge the ship to one-five-zero feet."

The Chief of the Watch reached for the handle of the diving klaxon. A strident alarm sounded throughout every space of the submarine. On the boat's 1MC he announced, "Dive! Dive!"

With all masts and antenna lowered except the Number Two scope, the *Oklahoma City* submerged beneath the waves until she was one hundred and fifty feet below the storm-tossed surface. Some of the strain eased from Coe's face.

The OOD looked aft first and reported, "after group venting," as he looked for the blast of air escaping the after main ballast tank vent group. Then he turned forward and reported, "forward group venting."

The ship's trim was tweaked until she was perfectly balanced 'trim sat' and sailing in the silent, eerie calm of the deep.

"Navigator, steer course two-seven-zero, slow ahead. Make your depth three-two-eight feet and deploy the TB-16 towed array."

The thin-lined towed array was a cluster of sophisticated sonar hydrophones that were strung at the end of an eight-hundred-yard-long cable behind the boat to allow the vessel's sonar system to listen for approaching enemy submarines. Coe waited for the towed array to deploy. The flotilla of surface ships he was escorting to the Celebes Sea would depart Guam at midnight. Until then it was *Oklahoma City's* mission to protect the waters west of the harbor against a possible attack by Chinese submarines that might have been alerted to the convoy's imminent departure.

"Towed array deployed, sir."

Coe nodded. He was about to leave the conn and return to his cabin to review his mission orders when a man in the control party noticed one of the boat's depth gauges had failed to track. For a moment there was a spike of alarm around the control room until the Chief of the Watch reached up and opened a large valve above his head that controlled the water input into the bank of depth gauges. The valve turned in his hand two times until it was all the way open. A moment later the needle on the gauge shifted and began to track. Furious, his face dark with thunder, the COW reached for a book by the ship's control panel and ran his finger down the line up sheet until he found the name and signature of the Ensign responsible for 'rigging the Forward Compartment Upper Level (FCUL) for dive'.

Coe turned and his eyes locked on the XO. "Mr Wickham, I want the man responsible for this oversight outside my cabin door in three minutes."

"Aye, sir," Richard Wickham growled, the promise of retribution the guilty man would receive implicit in his savage tone.

'Rig for Dive' was a critical part of every submarine's underway preparations. Before the boat submerged each valve directly connected to sea water systems or important to diving is first checked by an enlisted man, and then by one of the submarine's commissioned officers. It was a critical part of each submarine's procedures and the breech was serious. The

XO stormed from the conn in search of the offending Ensign. Thin-lipped and quietly seething, Chris Coe waited for exactly three minutes and then headed for his cabin.

*

The Ensign stood with his back pressed against the darkened upper-level passageway bulkhead outside the Captain's stateroom. The lights in the narrow corridor were red but even the dull glow could not hide the white-blanched features of the hapless junior officer's face. His eyes were brimming tears, his mouth tight and his lower lip trembling. Standing beside him, hands on hips and his face pressed close, Richard Wickham seethed in a towering rage.

Coe appeared at the end of the passage and the torrent of criticism being fired at the Ensign ended abruptly. "I'm not finished with you. Not by a long way, sailor." Wickham snarled off a final savage warning and then acknowledged the Captain with a curt nod and jabbed his thumb into the Ensign's chest.

"Ensign McCluskey, sir."

Coe stopped in front of his cabin door and stood toe-to-toe with the young officer. His face was hard, his eyes like black stone. Ensign McCluskey's hands began to shake. He tried to cringe away but there was nowhere to move. Coe looked the Ensign up and down carefully for a long moment before speaking.

"Do you understand the critical importance of rigging the Forward Compartment Upper Level for dive, Ensign McCluskey?"

"Yes… yes, sir," the young officer stammered.

"Do you understand how your inattention to your duty could have put every one of your shipmates lives at risk?" Coe put a stern unsympathetic tone to his voice.

"Yes, sir."

"Do you understand that your recklessness directly put the ship at risk?"

McCluskey lowered his head and his cheeks flushed red with shame. "Yes, sir," the voice was small and cowered.

Coe grunted, then narrowed his eyes. "Is there anything – anything at all I can say to you right now that will make you feel worse than the ass-chewing you have already received from the XO?"

The young officer blinked, gnawed his lip, then shook his head sorrowfully. "I apologize, sir. I promise to re-double my efforts to become a better officer, and re-double my attention to details, sir."

"Very well," Coe said. "You're dismissed. But remember this; Rig for Dive is a test of your word as a man and an officer. It's your reputation on the line. You are the one saying the ship is safe. If your word cannot be trusted, you cannot be trusted…"

Ensign McCluskey blinked again then scampered away down the passage. Now it was Wickham's turn to look at Coe with bewildered accusation in his eyes. He voiced his opinion stubbornly.

"Sir, at the very least, he'll have to be disqualified for Rig for Dive."

"No," Coe made a gut-instinct decision. "He's been disgraced. Everyone in the wardroom already knows he failed. That's punishment enough."

"Sir?"

"You heard me XO. The matter is closed," Coe said with finality.

Wickham gave a curt nod of his head, his temper still seething and prowled away down the passage. Coe remained in his cabin door, peering after the broad-shouldered silhouette of the XO, at a momentary loss to understand his own decision not to disqualify the young Ensign for Rig to Dive.

Was he losing his edge?

Were the Commodore's words already beginning to influence his rigid style of command?

Coe prided himself on running the smartest submarine in the fleet but in truth, he had always held a sympathetic fondness for the ship's crew. They were good people, hardworking and dedicated to their mission. They were all volunteers who breathed bad air and sometimes were forced to share a bed. They served because they were patriots – a point Coe never forgot. Some of the crew likened being submerged for weeks at a time to being in prison… except they got regular mail. But they endured the hardships and the challenges because they wanted to serve their country. The boat's seamen were an extension of their senior officers' thoughts and decisions, and therefore instruments of their will. It was the senior officers around him Coe struggled to trust; not because they were poor leaders but because he was an obsessive micromanager who felt the burden of his command like a leaden weight around his neck.

The sudden uncomfortable moment of self-realization shocked Chris Coe. He felt an impulsive uncharacteristic urge to follow the XO and explain his decision. He took a step into the passage and then steeled himself. Seeking sympathy or understanding were human frailties that an SSN Commander could not afford in the midst of a war. He gritted his teeth, returned to his cabin, and then decided this was no time to be alone when his thoughts were in rebellion. He pulled the cabin door shut behind him and prowled towards the conn, diverted from his path by a shuffle of movement and voices in sonar. He leaned his head through the darkened opening. Four operators sat in the gloom. "Something to report?"

The Sonar Supervisor on watch was a very capable First Class E-6. He looked up from a monitor, startled. The Captain's whispered nickname around the lower decks was 'Creeping Jesus'. He had an unnerving ability to ghost throughout the boat and arrive unexpected.

"Sir, First Class Petty Officer Gillard has picked up a faint transient," the Supervisor indicated the back of an operator who was perched hunch-shouldered over his console with headphones clamped to his ears. The operator's eyes were closed; his face creased with a frown of concentration. The man turned suddenly and whipped the headphones off, startled to see the Captain behind him.

"What have you got, son?"

"Something faint and probably mechanical, sir," the Petty Officer said. "I think it's metallic; some kind of grinding noise."

"A torpedo tube's outer doors?" the Supervisor asked sharply.

Gillard shook his head. "It's not as loud, and not as abrasive," he struggled to define the unfamiliar sound. The Supervisor snatched up the headphones and listened intently for sixty seconds, hearing nothing.

"You sure it's not a biologic?" Coe asked.

"Very sure, Captain."

"Could it be an underwater explosion, or a drilling rig?"

"No sir," the operator was adamant. "It's a mechanical transient of some kind."

Coe grunted. He exchanged glances with the Supervisor. The digital recording was rewound and then replayed. Coe heard it then too, and frowned. Coe didn't like mysteries and he didn't like surprises. He ran his eyes one last time across the sonar screens; there were no contacts, meaning the sound had most likely originated from an undetected underwater source. He stepped into the conn, closing the bi-fold sonar door behind him to maintain the darkened setting, and spoke quietly to the Officer of the Deck.

"OOD, slow to ahead one-third. Sonar is chasing the origin of an unknown transient, most probably mechanical. We need to bleed off some speed for a better listen."

The order was relayed to the Helm and a minute later the *OKC* began to slow through the ocean. Coe went back into sonar and stood, waiting.

It was a full five minutes before Petty Officer Gillard detected the sound again, this time so faintly that even on the playback, Coe could not pinpoint it amongst the background noise of the ocean. He looked to the Sonar Supervisor for a hint.

"I just don't know, sir," the Supervisor confessed. "I believe it's mechanical, but it's too intermittent to be anything typical we'd be familiar with."

"Could it have been a Chinese submarine opening its outer doors?" Coe asked the only question that mattered.

"The initial sounds Gillard detected could have been," the Supervisor admitted, although he was far from convinced. "But that doesn't explain the subsequent sounds, sir."

Again, Coe grunted. He was compelled to assume the entire Pacific Ocean west of Apra Harbor was hostile water, and that the threat from Chinese submarines against the surface fleet he was about to escort was real and imminent. But with nothing more to base his decision on, he knew that being drawn away from his position to investigate the noise further would put all three supply ships in danger. He looked down at his shoes for a long moment and folded his arms across his chest. There was no right answer.

"Keep your ears open, Sonar Sup," he addressed the Supervisor. "Let me know the moment you detect anything else. For now, we'll keep a close monitor but take no action." Then he glanced at his watch. It was 2300 hours. It would be another sixty tense minutes before the flotilla of supply ships would sail from Apra Harbor, and they could finally begin the perilous journey west.

*

In the quiet seclusion of his cabin, Chris Coe opened the laptop on his desk and began discussing the confidential details of their mission with Richard Wickham, laying out each of the components and contemplating the risks, dangers and challenges of every phase. The orders had been classified TS-SCI. (Top Secret – Sensitive Compartmented Information)

"Escorting the supply ships to the Celebes is not going to be a walk in the park, XO," Coe cautioned, "and I don't like the notion of being tethered to a surface convoy. It renders us vulnerable to attack if the Chinese can coordinate their boats to intercept us."

"Concur, sir," Wickham sat stiffly, unable to allow himself to relax in the Captain's presence for even a moment. "The best we can hope for is maybe sixteen knots from the tender, and the *Peary* and *Chambers* are Military Sealift Command vessels; I'm not sure how their civilian crews will measure up in a war zone."

Coe grunted to concede the point. The first leg of their mission was a journey of some fourteen hundred nautical miles west to the edge of the Celebes Sea, and even if the supply ships could maintain a fifteen-knot average speed, it was still almost four full days of hazardous sailing before the surface ships could be handed off to USS *Alexandria* (SSN-757). He thought for a moment and sighed. "Once we have the supply ships above us, we'll run north and take up station on the flank of the convoy. If the Chinese come hunting, it's most likely going to be from out of the Philippine Sea once we're out from under the cover of the Poseidons."

"Aye, sir." Wickham was about to venture an opinion when a sudden but respectful knock interrupted the meeting. The Weapons Officer leaned his head through the door.

Captain Coe looked up expectantly.

"Sir, all officers are mustered in the wardroom for the mission briefing as you requested."

"Very well, Weps. The XO and I will be there in a few minutes."

"Aye, sir."

After the lieutenant was gone, an abrupt mood-swing seemed to come over Chris Coe. For a long moment he sat in a tortured silence, conflicting emotions playing across his face.

Perhaps the Commodore was right – maybe I should loosen the reins and give my senior men more influence, more responsibility... but I can't now! Not when we're sailing towards the most dangerous mission we've ever embarked on. Perhaps, when the work is done; when the fighting is finished… maybe then I can start to trust, but not now. There are just too many lives at stake.

The Captain leaned forward and lowered his voice suddenly – and for a rare unfiltered moment the cloak of rank slid away and he was talking to Richard Wickham, man-to-man.

"Let me make myself clear, XO. It doesn't matter if you and I don't get along. It's not essential, or perhaps even preferable to the running of this boat. All that matters is that you understand me. I know you find your role frustrating at times, and I know my style of leadership is not particularly fashionable. But the fact is, Mister, that my responsibility to the Navy and to these sailors is to perform our mission successfully, and to bring every one home alive and in one piece. Your task is to maintain this boat on a fighting footing at all times and keep the men alert at their duties. If we fail this mission, it will be my responsibility. If men die, it will be my burden alone to bear. It's not a job I can share – so keep your mind focused on the only tasks that matter, and the things you can control. Understand?"

Richard Wickham flinched like he had been slapped across the face. There had been a callous and brutal tone in Coe's voice that had stung him. "Aye, sir," the XO's features turned to stone.

Wickham got to his feet and headed along the passageway for the wardroom. Coe closed the cabin door and leaned back against it. He screwed his eyes tightly shut and steeled his resolve and determination, then flung open the cabin door and followed the XO.

*

Access to the officers' staterooms and the wardroom was along the starboard side of the Middle Level Operations Compartment passageway, down a ladder from the Captain's stateroom and forward. On the port side of the passage were cramped crew berthings.

The small meeting room had been prepared in advance with special signs hanging outside the door and the 'bullseye' window covered over to indicate the sensitive nature of the classified discussion about to take place.

Coe and Wickham stepped into the wardroom and a voice called the Captain's arrival. "Attention on deck." The assembled officers straightened in their seats. There were nine chairs in the confined area nested around a large table and an additional large bench seat on the starboard side of the space. The inboard bulkhead contained storage cabinets and a long counter. The forward bulkhead featured a small bench and above the upholstered seat was perched a small locker packed with operating manuals and a small-screen TV set.

The Captain's position was at the head of the table with the seat to his right reserved for the XO. The Engineer sat to the Captain's left beside Weps and the Navigator. Coe nodded to his officers, then spoke briefly to the assembled group, outlining their mission, and then handed proceedings over to Richard Wickham. The XO went through the specifics of their secret mission in painstaking detail while Coe watched the slow-dawning realization spread across their faces. Some men's expressions became animated with boyish enthusiasm in the tense, electric silence. Other faces grew grave and troubled. The Navigator took over the briefing, first discussing the voyage plan and water management, and then revealing a large-scale chart showing the Philippines, Taiwan and the landmasses around the East China Sea and the Yellow Sea. On the chart he had projected a green line, illustrating their PIM (projected intended motion) track after they had rendezvoused with USS *Alexandria*. Several officers reached into their pockets for notebooks and began scribbling down key details, like students in a classroom. When the Nav finally fell silent, the Captain once again took over proceedings.

Chris Coe indicated the top of the green line that ended abruptly in the waters off Qingdao Harbor.

"Do not for one minute underestimate the enemy, or the enormity of the challenge we have been set," the line of Coe's mouth turned hard. "Qingdao is the headquarters port for the Chinese North Sea Fleet which also has primary bases and garrisons at Lushun, Lianyungang and Huludao. The North Sea Fleet's forces include three submarine flotillas, a destroyer flotilla, a landing ship flotilla, several speed boat flotillas and at least four, maybe five, sub-chaser squadrons. The Qingdao shipyard, located here, on the Shandong Peninsula," he described a small circle on the map to the south of the city, "specializes in constructing small patrol craft and landing ships. It's a major facility and the entire coastline is well protected by Naval Aviation facilities, meaning we can expect to sail into a hostile and alert environment."

When the meeting was over, Captain Coe cast a stern glance around the table, meeting each man's eye and fixing them all with the intensity of his gaze.

"Any questions or concerns?"

No one in the wardroom spoke.

"Beginning immediately, we will drill each section," Coe delivered his final message. "I want every man aboard alert and ready for action. Up until now our war has been a series of sudden savage knife-fights; random skirmishes that have been the consequence of fortune and fate," Coe said levelly. "Now we're sailing into the belly of the beast with one purpose and one purpose only; to hunt and to kill. For the first time we're going to take the war right to the enemy's doorstep and seize the initiative. If we're successful, we can alter the course of the war. It's that important."

*

The departure of the supply ships from Apra Harbor was delayed a full hour until the storm had passed across Guam Island and continued its track further east. By 0100 hours the skies overhead were clear and the seas abating. The wind dropped to a whisper and a P-8 Poseidon marine patrol aircraft was launched from Andersen Air Force Base to scour the ocean west of the harbor.

The three ships departed with USS *Emory S. Land* (AS-39) in the vanguard, USNS *Robert E Peary* (T-AKE-5) trailing in the submarine tender's wake, and USNS *Washington Chambers* (T-AKE-11) the last to depart. They steamed out into the black forbidding night with their navigation lights shuttered, making nine knots; dark grey slab-sided silhouettes beneath a cloud-shredded slice of pale moon.

Twenty miles west of Apra Harbor and at a depth of three-hundred-and-thirty feet, *Oklahoma City* continued to sail an aimless racecourse pattern, sanitizing the ocean for the threat of enemy submarines while Chris Coe raged and seethed with frustration about the delay.

Finally, a report from the sonar room confirmed the ships had cleared the harbor.

"Conn, sonar. Three new contacts bearing zero-nine-one, zero-nine-two and zero-eight-nine. It's the *Emory*, *Peary* and *Chambers* out of Guam. We also have a P-8 Poseidon overhead, bearing one-three-six and moving away."

"Sonar, aye," the OOD acknowledged the report and turned to where Chris Coe stood by the plot tables. *Oklahoma City* was in a 'modified battle stations' posture with a section tracking party in the control room, alert and anxious, ready for action at a moment's notice.

Coe nodded. "OOD, take us up to periscope depth so we can notify the flotilla of our position. Once they rendezvous, we'll break away from the convoy and take up a flanking station as they make their turn southwest."

"Aye, sir."

The mission had begun.

Oklahoma City was sailing back into harm's way.

*

The sudden jarring report over the submarine's 4MC emergency circuit brought sailors leaping from their bunks in the middle of the night.

"Emergency report! Emergency report! Fire in the Galley!"

The *Oklahoma City's* general alarm sounded and the OOD at the conn reacted instinctively, ordering the submarine towards the surface in case the boat needed to ventilate toxic fumes and smoke. "Dive, make your depth one-five-zero feet. Helm ahead one third. Sonar, clearing baffles to the right."

The COB relayed the order to the Diving Officer and a moment later the huge submarine began to tilt her nose towards the surface on a steady controlled ascent. Standing close to the plot table, Chris Coe clicked the timer on his stopwatch and then activated a speaker to monitor the flow of communication between the Galley and Damage Control Central, which aboard *Oklahoma City* was the CO's stateroom.

Richard Wickham had been asleep in his cabin when the fire alarm had sounded over the 4MC. He bounded out of bed, jolted awake and his adrenaline pumping. He flung open his cabin door and sprinted towards the galley. "Make a hole! Make a hole!" he shouted as he ran. The passageways were filled with sailors reporting to their emergency fire stations.

Wickham reached a crowded passageway forward of the Galley filled with enlisted men clutching EABs (Emergency Air Breather). From within the doorway of the Galley men waving grey blankets were simulating billowing smoke. Wickham barked a string of urgent orders and a masked fire team wearing FFE's (Fire Fighting Ensemble) and SCBA (Self Contained Breathing Apparatus) tanks came forward hauling a heavy hose between them.

Wickham strode to a nearby intercom handset. "Conn, this is the XO. I am in charge at the scene of the Galley fire. Heavy smoke. The fire is not out. Pressurize the hose!"

The fire team went aft, dragging the hose into the submarine's Galley while the alarms throughout the submarine continued their warbling blare until finally the firefighters re-emerged, having simulated containing the fire.

"Conn, XO," Richard Wickham pulled the cumbersome EAB from his face. He was sweating and breathing hard. "The fire in the Galley is out. Repeat. Fire in the Galley is out. The reflash watch is stationed. Heavy smoke. I recommend ventilating the ship."

Chris Coe had heard enough. He clicked off his stopwatch and looked at the time elapsed, his eyes hardening, the corners of his mouth turning down with bitterness. He picked up a handset. "XO, you were too damned slow! If that fire had been real, we'd all be dead by now. Do it again, and this time do it right. I want forty seconds shaved off your time, Mister!"

Richard Wickham said nothing.

08° 33' NORTH, 137° 41' EAST
PACIFIC OCEAN

Chapter 4:

Thirty-eight hours after departing Guam an alert sonarman aboard *Oklahoma City* detected a sound and raised the alarm, pointing to the green lines on the computer-like monitor at his work station. The Sonar Supervisor leaned over the young operator's shoulder, blinked, and then called the OOD.

"Conn, sonar. We are tracking a possible submerged contact, bearing two-nine-five. Blade rate details suggests it might be a Chinese submarine."

Chris Coe leaned in through the sonar shack door, his teeth gritted. The convoy of surface ships were steaming southwest at fourteen knots and were some two hundred nautical miles east of Palau, with *Oklahoma City* holding station ten miles to the north and operating at a depth of four hundred and forty feet.

"Any classification?" there was an edge of anxiety to the Captain's voice that he couldn't quite disguise.

The sonar operator's features were a mask of concentration. He looked bewildered and then disbelieving for a moment before he finally made a prognostication. "Sir, I think it's an old *Han*-class."

"Are you sure?" Coe didn't believe the diagnosis either. According to the latest US Intelligence sources, the Chinese only had three of the old first-generation nuclear attack submarines still in operation. And even if they had re-activated a couple of the decommissioned units, the reports suggested the *Han*-class boats would be kept close to Chinese waters – not sent roaming around the Pacific. The *Han* boats had been built based on 1950s technology; they were extremely noisy, had poor radiation shielding and carried a complement of largely outdated torpedoes.

The sonar operator bashed away at the keys of his console keyboard, waited while the submarine's sophisticated computer system analyzed the data, and then shrugged. "The system agrees, sir. It's a *Han*."

"Concur," the Sonar Sup agreed.

"Range?"

The Supervisor shook his head. "It could be anywhere up to fifty-thousand yards, sir – maybe as far away as two convergence zones. But my guess is that the enemy has detected, or been alerted to the position of the convoy. I don't think he knows we exist."

"Speed?"

The Sonar Supervisor checked. "Sixteen knots. He's closing. Sir, I'm designating Sierra Two-Four the *Han* Master Eleven."

Coe returned to the conn and ordered the stand-by fire-control tracking party to start working a solution to the target, and ordered the OOD to deploy the TB-29 thin-line towed array. The OOD ordered *Oklahoma City* into a series of course changes, trying to triangulate the position of the approaching enemy submarine.

It took several patient minutes with data pouring into the fire-control tracking party until finally they had a solution and approximate range. The *Han* was closing on the convoy, on a course to intercept the *Emory S. Land*.

"Officer of the Deck, bring us around to course two-eight-zero, decrease speed to five knots, maintain depth four-four-zero feet and man battle stations torpedo." Coe planned to lay in ambush and blindside the Chinese submarine as it closed on the convoy.

"Aye, sir," the OOD snapped crisply. "Helm all ahead one third, make turns for five knots. Dive, make your depth four-four-zero feet. Chief of the Watch, silently man battle stations."

Like most ships, *Oklahoma City* had developed a procedure for manning battle stations in close quarters without sounding the alarms. The submarine's emergency DC lights flashed three times. The men raced to their positions.

Coe turned to the Officer of the Deck. "OOD, make tubes one and two ready in all respects."

The game of cat and mouse had begun, with the three unsuspecting American supply ships as tempting bait…

*

The tense minutes of waiting dragged out, each second a test of patience and nerve. Coe stood quietly on the conn's raised section of the deck, his outward expression impassive and unaffected by the charged atmosphere in the control room, but behind his eyes his thoughts were fraught with anxiety and uncertainty.

He visualized the three-dimensional tactical situation; imagining the Chinese submarine approaching the unsuspecting convoy, and slowly passing across his bow from right to left while *Oklahoma City* lay silently in the depths, waiting to pounce. He tried to put himself in the shoes of the Chinese skipper; would he dash closer to launch his attack, falling on the tantalizing prize like a wolf, or would he make a cautious approach, wary of a trap? Coe dismissed the possibility that the *Han* commander would ascend to periscope depth to make his attack. Coming shallow would give the Chinese submarine commander a chance to choose his target from the flotilla of convoy vessels, but the trade-off would be speed. At periscope depth, Coe guessed the best the old Chinese nuc could do would be five knots. The flotilla would quickly steam out of range and disappear over the horizon.

Coe's hunch was that the Chinese Captain would be impulsive and that he would close on the convoy at good speed, staying deep and trying to position himself to take out all three ships in the flotilla before they could scatter across the ocean.

A sudden call from the sonar shack brought his mind jarring back into focus.

"Conn, sonar. Master Eleven is slowing. Screws making turns for eight knots. Transient sounds… he's opening his outer doors."

Coe nodded. "Fire control, range to target?"

"Eight thousand yards, sir."

"Do you have a firing solution, yet?"

"Yes, sir."

"Sonar, conn. Any sign Master Eleven is alerted?"

"Conn, sonar. No sir. He's tooling along, course unaltered…" the report from the sonar shack tailed off unexpectedly as though something had been left unsaid.

Coe was about to order the attack when the voice from the sonar room came again, this time loud with fresh urgency. "Conn, sonar! New contact, bearing two-nine-two! This is Sierra Two-Five. Based on tonal information, I'm classifying Sierra Two-Five designate Master Twelve. It's a Chinese *Shang*. It's been hiding in the noise of the *Han*."

"Sonar, conn. Range?" Coe snapped. He was seething.

"I'm guessing about twelve thousand yards, sir. He's been trailing the *Han*, cloaked in the noise of its baffles."

Coe thought fast. The *Shang* was a much more dangerous threat than the *Han*, but if he waited and attacked the *Shang*, the *Han* would pass by his bow and have an unobstructed run to the convoy, firing its torpedoes and savaging the surface ships from close range. But if he attacked the *Han*, he would reveal his position to the trailing *Shang* and *Oklahoma City* would be dead in the water.

"Fire control. Get me a solution on the *Shang*," Coe barked.

Richard Wickham began working slavishly over the submarine's billion-dollar fire control system, working a bracket of functions using the enemy submarine's bearing and bearing rate. The American Navy still used a sophisticated version of the Eklund Range algorithm developed back in the 1960s. The process required Coe to drive the submarine to 'drive the bearing rate'; changing *OKCs* speed across the line of the enemy submarine.

"Computer is chewing on it, sir," the XO, who was also the fire-control officer replied.

"Continue tracking Master Eleven," Coe growled, aborting the torpedo launch against the *Han*.

A fire-control watchstander tracking the bearing rate of the *Shang* noticed a sudden change and added his voice to the tension. "Possible target zig, Master Twelve."

Richard Wickham peered at the dot-stacker display. "Confirm target zig! Looks like the *Shang* is pulling out of Master eleven's baffles and making his own attack run at the convoy."

Coe's mind raced to recalculate the sudden scenario change and then took the best of the bad options available to him.

"Attention in Control. We are tracking two Chinese submarines, the *Han* Master Eleven, and the *Shang* Master Twelve. I want to engage the *Han* first from tube one with minimum enabable distance. We will shoot and cut the wire. Immediately we will engage the *Shang* with tube two and once we have a good wire, we'll clear datum at standard. Any questions or concerns?" He swung his eyes around the control room like he was sighting the twin barrels of a shotgun.

No one spoke.

"Very well. Carry on," Coe's voice then took on a new and determined tone. "Fire control. Fire point procedures Master Eleven, the *Han*. Tube one, single ADCAP torpedo."

"Ship ready," the OOD said.

"Solution ready," the FCC said a moment later.

"Weapons ready," Weps confirmed.

"Shoot on generated bearings, tube one, Master Eleven!"

"Shoot on generated bearings, tube one, Master Eleven, aye!" the XO's voice was charged with tension.

The Mk 48 ADCAP launched from tube one with a whoosh and liquid pulse of energy that seemed to shudder the submarine.

"Fire control. Fire point procedures Master Twelve, the *Shang*. Tube two, single ADCAP torpedo!"

"Aye, sir!" Richard Wickham's voice echoed the instruction. "Firing tube two at *Shang* Master Twelve!"

Three seconds later tube two launched its torpedo and again the *Oklahoma City* seemed to almost recoil in the water from the tremendous rush of energy expelled.

"Conn, sonar. Weapons running normal."

"Cut the wires to torpedoes one and two. Close outer doors!" Coe snapped. It was a risk, but a calculated one; without their wire guided tethers back to the submarine the Mk 48s were running free across the ocean, but at such close range and with such a clear solution to both enemy submarines, the Mk 48s were almost assured of hits.

"OOD, make our course two-nine-five." Coe spoke calmly. *OKC* had a good solution to the *Han* and he had used a very short enabling range on the Mk 48; he knew the enemy submarine would be quickly detected by the torpedo he had fired and would hone in on its prey immediately. Coe held his nerve and waited, knowing that once the *Shang* became alerted to *OKCs* presence the enemy commander would most likely fire a snap-shot back along the bearing.

"Aye, sir!" the OOD snapped, caught up, like every man in the conn, by the tension and imminent threat of the Chinese submarines. The orders were barked, and the *Oklahoma City* turned further to the north. Coe's plan was to lead the Chinese submarines away from the flotilla of surface ships, giving them time to clear the contact point and scatter across the ocean.

"Conn, sonar. Master Eleven changing course and increasing speed. She's turning away from us, sir. Master Twelve alerted. He's firing noise makers and accelerating."

"Transients?" Coe asked. "Is Master Twelve flooding his tubes?" It was the *Shang* that Coe feared most.

"Conn, sonar. Hard to tell, sir. There's too much noise to be certain."

Coe bit his lip, trying to make complex mathematical calculations in his mind. "Fire control. Time to acquisition tube one Master Eleven?" he fired the question, even though the information was being displayed on screens at the conn.

It was an impossible question for Wickham to answer accurately. Both enemy submarines had made radical course and speed changes. He gave Coe his best estimates. "Time to acquire the *Han* Master Eleven approximately six minutes, sir. Time to acquire Master Twelve, seven minutes thirty seconds."

Coe said nothing.

Six minutes. It was a long time to wait with your life – and the lives of every man aboard – hanging precariously in the balance. Beneath his shirt, Coe felt himself beginning to sweat; chill little beads of perspiration trickling down his back. The silence across the conn became almost eerie. They were waiting, and subconsciously every man stole a glance overhead as if they might sense danger approaching.

"Conn, sonar! Transients. Master Twelve has opened his outer doors!"

Coe said nothing. The *Shang* commander, aware that an American torpedo was homing inexorably towards his submarine was fighting back.

"Torpedo in the water!" The *Shang* had fired a snap-shot down the bearing of the Mk 48. "Approaching at thirty-six knots and accelerating, bearing two-five-five. I think it's a Yu-6."

Coe flicked through what he knew about the enemy torpedo. The Yu-6 was the Chinese counterpart of the Mk 48 and could either be guided by wire, active and passive homing, or wake homing. It was claimed the Chinese reverse-engineered the design for the weapon after an American Mk 48 was reportedly recovered by Chinese fishermen back in the 80s. Coe doubted the torpedo hunting him would be wire guided. The Chinese boat had made a radical course change the moment his Mk 48 went active. Most likely he had fired intuitively, then cut the wires and begun evasion maneuvers. But that didn't negate the danger approaching *Oklahoma City*.

"OOD, make our course zero-nine-zero," Coe said. "Increase to flank speed."

It was possible the *Oklahoma City* could outrun the enemy torpedo if it could keep enough distance between itself and the weapon until the Chinese Yu-6 simply ran out of fuel and sank harmlessly to the ocean floor.

"Time to acquisition *Han* Master Eleven?"

"Two minutes to Master Eleven. Three minutes thirty to Master Twelve," Richard Wickham replied instantly as though he had been anticipating the question.

The *Oklahoma City* changed course and surged ahead to flank speed. Coe glanced at his wristwatch, and it seemed like the second hand had frozen. Then his eyes found the old analogue compass rose at the forward end of the conn in the overhead. He could see the bearing of the incoming torpedo and his heading. In a control room filled with digital readouts and flat-panel screens, it was a sobering touchstone of reality for a man like Chris Coe.

The precarious waiting game continued. Coe resisted the temptation to fire countermeasures now that he had started evasion maneuvers and left datum. It was still possible the Chinese torpedo could get lost at datum and be rendered harmless. If that happened, any countermeasures he fired might alert the enemy torpedo's sensors and actually lead the weapon directly towards him. Coe was still unsure whether the *Shang* had detected *OKC* through its towed array or whether the Chinese Captain had merely fired his torpedo down the bearing. If it had been a snap shot along the bearing, Coe didn't want to reveal *OKC's* location – unless the inbound torpedo suddenly acquired.

He waited, fighting against the urge to fidget while the *OKC* surged at high speed, putting distance between himself and his firing point, gently adjusting course to keep the enemy torpedo close to the edge of his starboard baffles so the men in the sonar shack could continue to pass along any torpedo bearing changes.

Sixty long seconds later the conn open mic speaker burst to life.

"Conn, sonar. The Yu-6 has locked on and has just gone active. I have a high SNR and constant bearing and a shift to a short pulse length. Torpedo is on our tail and homing! Speed forty-two knots."

"Launch countermeasures!" Coe fired the order. "OOD, make our course zero-nine-zero! Smartly!"

"Aye sir! Launching countermeasures. Making my course zero-nine-zero."

The instructions were repeated crisply by the Chief of the Boat. Two ADC Mk3 tubes were launched. The decoys activated immediately, radiating a frenzy of noise into the ocean.

"Fish tail the rudder fifteen degrees." Coe was thinking fast. Fish tailing the boat's rudder was, in essence, an additional cheap countermeasure technique that would create a huge cloud of water bubbles and disturbed ocean for the Chinese torpedo to home on. Once the maneuver was completed Coe ordered, "Take charge of your helm!"

Oklahoma City turned due east at flank speed.

Coe wondered whether he had done enough.

Only time would tell…

*

"Conn, sonar! Explosion in the water, bearing two-six-five, range nine thousand yards. Breaking up noises on the bearing of the *Han*."

An impulsive cheer rang out around the control room. Coe gritted his teeth but let the chorus of voices wash around the room. The frivolity of the celebration irritated him. It lasted for just a few seconds before the sonar shack was back on comms.

"Conn, sonar," it was the Sonar Supervisor's voice, flushed with relief. "The *Shang's* torpedo has fallen for one of the noisemakers. It is no longer trailing."

"Sonar, aye," Coe acknowledged the order. With the Chinese torpedo decoyed the knife-fight changed momentum again. "Officer of the Deck, slow speed to ahead one third. Come right to two-one-zero and make your depth six-three-zero feet."

The *Shang* was still somewhere beyond them in the depths of the ocean with the *OKC's* Mark 48 closing inexorably on its tail. But if the Chinese skipper somehow managed to evade the threat, Coe wanted to be prepared to fire again immediately.

"Weps," the Captain turned to the submarine's Weapons Officer. "Reload and make full ready tubes one and two."

"Aye, sir," Weps repeated the order.

The order was more easily given than accomplished. Reloading three-thousand-pound torpedoes into their launch tubes took time. Each Mk 48 in the torpedo room lay on a skid, and the rounds were moved port and starboard via hydraulic rails. Once in the reload position, each weapon was hooked to a ram, then the door opened, and the torpedo sent into the tube on rollers. Once safely inside the tube, a TMD (Torpedo Mounted Dispenser) wire holder was locked to the inside of the door, the wire threaded through the door, and then the door finally shut. Because the boat was at battle stations, a handful of *OKC's* qualified machinists from the nuc plant were working side-by-side with the submarine's torpedomen to increase efficiency.

"Conn, sonar. *Shang* Master Twelve has just released a noisemaker... and a second one. He's violently maneuvering and cavitating."

Coe tried to visualize the three-dimensional battlefield while the fire control team dealt with the data pouring in to the BSY-1 fire control system; using the information to keep a constantly updated firing solution. The work was technical and demanding... and unnecessary.

The Mk 48 hunting the *Shang* was using its powerful active seeker as it reached the terminal phase of its pursuit. The American torpedo slammed straight through the string of Chinese noisemakers undeterred. Forty seconds later the sounds of an almighty explosion reached the *OKC* as the Mk 48's six-hundred-and-fifty pound high-explosive warhead detonated on impact. The force of the monstrous underwater detonation tore a hole in the Chinese submarine and wrenched the hull open, cleaving the enemy boat into two pieces. The aftershock washed over the *OKC* like the tremor of an earthquake, heaving books from their shelves, causing light fixtures to break, and shaking a hazy cloud of dirt and dust down from the overhead.

"Conn, sonar. Explosion in the water, bearing one-nine-zero. The *Shang* took a direct hit and she's breaking up. I have air noises from rupturing tanks and a secondary explosion, probably from the stricken steam plant." Another sudden spontaneous cheer rippled around the conn. This time Coe indulged the celebration without visible signs of annoyance as it undulated around him.

"COB, maintain battle stations until we can complete a careful search of the area to make sure all enemy targets have been eliminated. I also want to confirm there isn't another threat lurking in wait," he paused impatiently until the cheering stopped and order had been restored. "Take us up to periscope depth. We need to get a message to Guam, and we need to re-gather our flock of surface vessels."

As the submarine began to rise towards the surface, Chris Coe snatched for the 1MC. "Attention battle stations party," his voice was flat and matter-of-fact. "It appears we have successfully engaged the *Han* and *Shang*, and they have both been sunk. We are reloading now, and after a search of the area, we will transition to section tracking party. We are currently on our way to PD to make an engagement report to Task Force." Coe could have said more; he could have congratulated the crew for their effort; sang their praises for a task efficiently handled. Instead, he strode from the conn without another word leaving Richard Wickham and the Chief of the Boat bewildered and bitterly disappointed.

*

Richard Wickham knocked politely, then waited for Chris Coe to beckon him before he dared open the Captain's cabin door. Coe was seated at his desk; his laptop open and a sheaf of reports and paperwork awaiting his attention. Wickham sat at the seat beside the desk like a patient in a doctor's surgery.

Coe continued to work; a pair of silver-rimmed spectacles perched on the end of his nose as he two-finger typed. The fraught silence lasted a full two minutes before the Captain closed the laptop and turned. He sat back in the seat, as though trying to keep his distance from the XO.

"You held a drill-team debriefing in the wardroom, XO?"

"Yes, sir," Wickham said. "The drill team mustered and Senior Lieutenant Parsons lead the critique. We reviewed the actions of the recent Galley fire drill. Based on your comment when the drill was completed and the time taken, it was deemed unsatisfactory and a series of steps have been put in place to streamline our fire team response. I'm confident that next time the drill is performed, the men will respond with greater efficiency."

Coe said nothing. Instead, he cast a casual glance over a bank of bulkhead-mounted gauges and dials. *Oklahoma City* was cruising due west at fifteen knots, positioned three-hundred-and-sixty-feet below the surface, and on station to the north of the convoy of supply ships.

"The fire control team worked well under your supervision during our engagement with the two Chinese submarines," Coe admitted grudgingly, "although I find the cheering a little unseemly. You might want to have a quiet word to the men about it in future. I appreciate the impulse to celebrate the destruction of an enemy target, but the control room is not the place for that kind of ill-discipline aboard my boat. I've tolerated it up until now. I'd like it to stop."

"Aye, sir. I'll see to it," Wickham's features tightened, taking the criticism personally.

"And I'd like you to run another 'angles and dangles' exercise. I know we exercised after leaving Guam, but if we continue to contact and engage enemy submarines, our stowage must be ship-shape at all times. See to it."

"Aye, sir," Wickham nodded through gritted teeth. The XO believed there was a danger in exercising the crew and the ship too frequently. The men aboard were all well-trained and ready to fulfill their new mission. They had been at sea for several weeks prior to returning to Guam, and now they were back at sea again. They were all on the edge of excellence and overtraining might abrade their alertness. There was also a genuine danger that a drill could inadvertently damage equipment on the ship; something innocuous caused by gear degenerizing or something as significant as the towed arrays streaming from the stern of the boat that might be affected by slowing and speeding rapidly. To Wickham's mind, the only drills necessary now that they were sailing into harm's way were section drills on 'snap shots' – the code word to rapidly shoot if an enemy threat is detected and warranted an immediate response. But rather than voice his concerns, the XO obediently nodded. "I'll arrange another 'angles and dangles' exercise immediately, sir."

"Very good," Coe's features were pinched. He felt stifled in the XO's presence, aware of the tension that bristled between them but equally aware that he did not have the people-skills or the desire to bridge the gap – despite the Commodore's pointed advice. Coe believed that discipline, above all else, mattered most. Commanding a nuclear attack boat wasn't a popularity contest – it was a constant challenge and test of his will. Of course, he had heard the whispers, muttered behind closed doors when he had stridden the passageways. He knew there were elements of the crew that resented his iron rule and others that believed he had ice-water running through his veins; the criticism delivered with a hushed mix of outraged and awed whispers.

Richard Wickham got suddenly to his feet. The Captain said nothing. Instead, Chris Coe turned his attention to the stack of paperwork and reports at his elbow. The XO left without another word, closing the cabin door silently behind him. Coe listened to the XO's footsteps receding along the passageway.

*

The sudden announcement over the submarine's 1MC was loud and blaring, startling Chris Coe from a fitful sleep.

"The ship will be conducting an 'angles and dangles' exercise," Richard Wickham warned, his voice carrying to every space aboard *OKC*.

Coe lay in his bunk, exhaustion fogging his thoughts, and felt the *OKC* gradually accelerate. It was unusual for him to stay in his rack during a drill or exercise, but he had done so deliberately as a way to subtly make his displeasure with his senior officers known. The bed beneath him tilted perilously as the submarine put its snub nose down and began to dive at a twenty-degree angle. The maneuver lasted almost two minutes before the deck finally leveled off and then began to rise again. The angle was equally steep, this time the submarine ascending at speed. Fittings in the Captain's cabin creaked and a stack of books on their shelf swayed. The submarine came up from the depths silently, not even her hull popping at the dramatic change in water pressure.

When *Oklahoma City* was again level at one-hundred-and-fifty-feet, the entire process was repeated at a twenty-five-degree angle. The exercise tested the ship's readiness for sea and replicated the extreme maneuvers that might be necessary in a combat situation. Success was largely the responsibility of the submarine's Chiefs for it was the Chief of the Boat who had confirmed the ship was rigged for sea when *OKC* had departed Guam.

At a thirty-degree angle, the deck pitched down so acutely that it was necessary for everyone aboard to clutch at a handhold to maintain their balance. The submarine reached a depth of eight hundred feet and began to rise once more. From the Galley, aft, Chris Coe heard a stack of crockery smash, and then from somewhere beyond his closed cabin door a heavy object crashed to the deck making a sound so loud that Richard Wickham and the COB in the control room both physically cringed.

Coe flung himself from his bunk in a rage and dressed quickly. His hair was tousled and his face haggard with exhaustion as he stormed into the control room, moving from hand-hold to hand-hold to maintain his balance. *Oklahoma City* was rising steeply through three hundred feet on her way back up to periscope depth. Coe glared around the room, the sterile light making him blink owlishly.

"XO, secure from 'angles and dangles' immediately. Clearly you and the Chief of the Boat need to work on our rig-for-sea," he understated the obvious, his voice a sullen irritated growl. "If this had been a close combat situation, the noise through this ship could have resulted in our position being given away. And if it had happened when we were fighting the *Shang*, we could all be dead, damn it." He turned on the COB then, his eyes blazing. "Chief I want every space on this ship re-stowed immediately and then I want the entire 'angles and dangles' exercise repeated until the stowage is right."

Coe stormed from the control room in a thunderous mood leaving a pall of gloom and uncomfortable silence in his wake. Two hours later the angles exercise was repeated to the Captain's satisfaction.

*

The *Oklahoma City* rendezvoused with the USS *Alexandria* in deep water north of Karakelong Island on the eastern edge of the Celebes Sea. The journey from Guam had taken almost four days. The surface ships arrived an hour after the two submarines by which time the *Alexandria* had already begun delousing the *OKC* in preparation for her perilous trek north into Chinese-occupied waters.

The delousing process took ninety minutes of patient, precise navigation and a flurry of messages between the two

SSNs via the ship-board UQC underwater telephone, once more commonly known as the Gertrude.

Delousing was a process devised by the American submarine force to check vessels for transient rattles prior to going on station, with *Oklahoma City* sailing straight lines at a constant speed and depth while *Alexandria* monitored, using her vast array of sophisticated sensors to detect any transient noises being emanated from the boat it was trailing.

When the delicate process was complete, the two fast attack boats passed each other a final time at slow speed and at an agreed depth separation, less than a thousand yards of ocean dividing them.

"Joe, we appreciate the check-up," Coe snatched up a phone receiver at the conn, depressed the Transmit trigger, and thanked the commander of USS *Alexandria* over the Gertrude. "The convoy is now yours, buddy. Safe trip into the South China Sea."

"Thanks Chris," Commander Joseph Whalam's voice was loud and distorted through the surrounding ocean. "Good luck to you. Godspeed and good hunting."

Coe hung up the Gertrude and turned to the XO. There was a brittle thin smile on his lips that Wickham had rarely seen before. "The breakaway song, please, Mister Wickham."

"Aye, sir," Wickham joined in the brief moment of levity and actually smiled. He couldn't remember the last time he had done that. Thirty seconds later the ocean around USS *Alexandria* boomed the opening lines of a famous Johnny Paycheck song, *'Take this job and shove it – I ain't workin' here no more'*, as USS *Oklahoma City* turned north-northwest and set a course towards the Yellow Sea, almost two thousand nautical miles away.

Forty minutes later Coe was in his stateroom when the 21MC speaker above his head squawked to life. *Oklahoma City* had risen to periscope depth and deployed a floating wire antenna, with the line trailing on the surface of the ocean to clear incoming broadcast data.

"Captain, Navigator," the Lieutenant Commander's voice announced. "We've just received the regular eleven-thirty Zulu message traffic, including a message from *Alexandria* to SUBPAC confirming *OKC* had no detectable noise sources or rattles during delousing."

Chapter 5:

With *OKC* on a course for the Yellow Sea and sailing in deep water at sixteen knots the atmosphere aboard the submarine changed noticeably. Now the ship was untethered from convoy duty, a sense of new purpose charged the air. Chris Coe noticed the new alacrity with which orders were carried out and the grim focus of the men in the conn as they went about their work routines. It was the same throughout the entire length and breadth of the boat; equipment was checked, torpedoes tested and diagnosed for faults, engine equipment was stripped down and serviced – as if everyone aboard understood the importance of their mission and the need for the boat to be fully operational.

Coe paced the conn and the passageways, restless with tension behind a stony façade. Everything that could be done was being attended to, yet still he felt apprehensive. The Chief of the Boat caught the Captain in his cabin re-reading the mission orders and knocked politely.

"Enter," Coe shut the computer down.

Chief of the Boat, Nathan Simpkins shuffled through the door, stiff and awkward with discomfort.

"You need something, COB?" Coe removed his spectacles and set them on the small desk. His face was haggard, the lines around his eyes and at the corners of his mouth deeply etched by fatigue.

"Yes, sir," Simpkins said.

Coe leaned back in his chair and studied the Chief of the Boat carefully. Simpkins was a year younger than Coe, and the second oldest man aboard the submarine. He had been *Oklahoma City's* COB for the past two years and was good at his job. He had wavy black hair, the hard-working features of a truck driver or a mechanic, and a broad New Orleans accent. The Captain nodded. "Take a seat and tell me what's on your mind."

The Chief of the Boat was the senior enlisted man aboard the submarine. By assignment his task was to be the conduit between the boat's crew and the officers of the wardroom;

comparable to a Command Master Chief aboard an American Navy surface ship. Typically, they were prickly, outspoken survivors with a borderline belligerent attitude – but Nathan Simpkins was not cast from that mould.

Traditionally the link between the Commander and the COB aboard a submarine was a strong one; it was in the interests of both men to work well together. But for Chris Coe, the relationship with Nathan Simpkins had always been strained. Coe readily accepted responsibility for the tension, rarely confiding in the COB or seeking out his advice on crew matters.

"Well, sir," Simpkins flustered, feeling acutely embarrassed. Coe was staring at him woodenly. "I mean no disrespect, but I feel you have a right to know that there's some resentment starting to ferment within the boat's crew," he got the words out at last and made a fretful face.

"Resentment?" Coe was instantly on guard. His eyes turned hard and searching. "What kind of resentment – exactly, COB?"

Simpkins shifted on his seat and then steeled himself now that the worst of the exchange was over. "Some of the men are bitter. The feeling is that you're driving the crew too hard. They've worked their asses off and instead of a word of praise, you're driving them even harder."

"And this is coming from the Goat Locker, COB?" Coe's voice pitched low.

"It's not just the Chiefs, sir," now that he had delivered the news, the Chief of the Boat became more assured. "It's the enlisted men too."

The Goat Locker was the compartment where the Chief Petty Officers slept, located on the mid-level of the submarine on the starboard side.

Coe felt a stab of betrayal; a rebuke that brought a flush of hot color to his cheeks. For a long moment he said nothing, his eyes focussed on a point on the bulkhead above the COB's head while he wrestled with his emotions.

To fill the awkward bristling silence, Nathan Simpkins blurted, "Sir, you have good officers and a great, hard-working crew. They deserve to be encouraged for their efforts."

Chris Coe leaned forward in his chair suddenly and his expression turned dark and stormy. "COB, listen to me carefully. I am running a warship, not a pleasure cruise and this is not an exercise. We are at war! Men's lives are at stake, and I take that responsibility very, very seriously. This might be the modern American Navy, but this is my boat, damn it. I'm not handing out certificates and medals to crewmen and officers for participation. The reward will be successfully completing our mission and getting these young men home in one piece. Do you understand me?"

"Yes, sir," Simpkins stiffened. A flush of hot color rose up around the collar of his shirt. "I understand perfectly."

"Good," Coe swung away, seething. "And the next time you hear someone sulking about not being appreciated, you tell them they should have joined the Air Force."

Nathan Simpkins got to his feet, suddenly impatient to flee the room. Coe reached for the stack of paperwork at his elbow. "You're dismissed, COB."

*

The wardroom table was set for dinner with a blue tablecloth bearing the boat's name embroidered on one edge, and the table set with porcelain plates, glasses and two pitchers; one containing water and the other containing concentrated juice, affectionately known by officers and crew as 'bug juice'. The assembled officers were standing behind their chairs, waiting for Chris Coe to arrive. After several uncertain minutes a mess specialist entered the wardroom.

"XO, the Captain has been delayed a few minutes. He suggested you men begin the evening meal without him, sir."

Outwardly the faces around the table remained impassive, but inwardly most of the assembled officers were thankful for the brief respite. They sat and the mess steward re-entered the room bearing bowls of soup which he served in strict formal order. The officers applied themselves to the soup in silence, studiously bent over their bowls while baskets of warm bread were brought to the table.

As the mess steward began clearing away the bowls Chris Coe suddenly entered the room, pre-empting the officers who had instinctively begun rising from their seats. "As you were," he said, waving them back down.

Coe took his seat at the head of the table and swung his eyes around the room, searching each man's face as though he were trying to identify the Judas amongst them. His eyes settled on the Nav, who frowned and looked down at his empty soup bowl. The atmosphere in the room changed as though an icy blast of air had swept through the room.

Coe sat in silence until the dishes that comprised the main meal were set in the center of the table and the mess specialists removed the soup bowls. Once the mess specialist had left the wardroom, Coe waited until the food had been passed around family-style and each man's plate was full.

"It's tradition for discussions during these evening meals to be about anything other than our mission," the Captain said slowly as all eyes around the table turned to him. He held their gaze levelly, his features like stone so that no one was aware of the simmering betrayal he still felt after his meeting with Nathan Simpkins. "But I'm going to make an exception this evening. XO, you can leave the quote log in the locker. There'll be nothing amusing said tonight and nothing I say can leave this room – do you all understand?"

Heads nodded and again the atmosphere in the wardroom changed. Now the air was suddenly thick with tension and anticipation. The food on each man's plate slowly congealed and went cold as Chris Coe outlined the details of their mission.

In careful, patient tones he described their intended attack on the Chinese military convoy, the need for absolute stealth when they steamed close to the coast of China, the importance of laying off Qingdao Harbour and monitoring ship movements until *Minnesota* and *Colorado* made the rendezvous and the attack was initiated. He stressed the sensitive nature of the arms shipment the Chinese convoy would be carrying and the possibility that the weapons being carried were on their way to Pakistan to coax that nation into the world war.

When he finished the officers around the table sat in stunned, troubled silence. Only the Nav and XO had any inkling of how grave and how fraught with danger their mission was. Coe saw the sober expressions on his officers' faces and felt grimly satisfied.

Perhaps now they would understand why he was driving the boat and the crew and every one of them so hard, he mused bitterly.

"I'm not going to ask if there are any questions. I've told you all I can. But if you have any comments, feel free to speak up."

He searched the faces of the men around him again. The mood was almost funereal. "Very well," he got abruptly to his feet. "Enjoy the rest of your meal gentlemen, and from now until we tie up again at Apra Harbor, keep your mind on your mission. There's no room aboard this boat for sensitive feelings when lives are at stake. Any man not sure he can perform his work at the level of excellence I expect can visit me in my cabin later this evening. That will give me time to arrange a replacement for you before we sail into the Yellow Sea."

*

As *Oklahoma City* reached the southern edge of the Yellow Sea, the submarine began to slow from sixteen knots to twelve, and then from twelve to five knots as she crept towards Qingdao Harbor. Coe had ordered the submarine rigged for Ultra-Quiet by signalling two flashes on the DC lights and then the word was passed around on the internal phones. Now the ship's nonessential equipment was secured, the fan speed for the ventilation system reduced, and all her watertight doors were on the latch to prevent the sound of their opening and closing from transmitting out into the ocean. The submarine's routine maintenance projects were paused and the crew, sensing the moment, moved quietly as ghosts as they went about their tasks.

Seven nautical miles off Qingdao the Captain ordered the boat to periscope depth. It was a few minutes before sunrise. *OKC's* periscope would break the surface with the rising sun behind it.

Oklahoma City came up from the depths very slowly, turning a full circle to clear her baffles as she ascended. As she came shallow, the voice of the Diving Officer intoned, "Passing two hundred... passing one-seventy..."

The OOD spoke next. "Captain the ship is at one-five-zero feet. I have cleared baffles and hold no sonar contacts. Request permission to go to periscope depth on course two-six-five, sir."

"Very well, proceed to periscope depth."

The *Oklahoma City* rose up from the ocean with only the Number Two scope raised. The moment the scope broke the surface the OOD said quickly, "No close contacts."

"No threat ESM contacts," the ESM technicians in their space behind the conn announced over the open mic. "Request raise the ESM mast."

"Raise the ESM mast," the Officer of the Deck ordered. Chris Coe felt a sudden flutter of anxiety and crushed down on the emotion.

"Raise the ESM, aye, sir," the order was echoed. The Chief of the Watch responded, working the controls on the Ballast Control Panel.

The slender mast rose and began feeding information to the ship. The control board at an electronic-warfare technician's station lit up immediately.

"Multiple electronic source activity, Captain," the operator said. "A mix of UHF chatter and some VHF stuff as well. It's Chinese, sir," he stared at the data coming in from the BLQ-10 receiver.

"Sonar, conn. Report all contacts."

"Conn, sonar. I have multiple Broad Band contacts, bearing two-seven-five, sir. Best guess is that there is commercial traffic but as far as I can tell, it's a good distance away."

"Conn, aye," Coe said. It would make sense, he reasoned. Qingdao Harbor would be packed with small and large commercial vessels, many of them now operating in the service of the Chinese war effort – including those ships in the convoy he had been sent to destroy. In peacetime the harbor was one of the ten busiest commercial ports in the world with thousands of small and large ship movements each day.

Periscope depth for a *Los Angeles*-class attack submarine like *Oklahoma City* was officially sixty-two feet. Coe waited until the boat leveled.

"Raise the periscope."

The periscope assistant worked the operating ring to raise the periscope, then snapped the handles into place as it rose out of the well. The XO stepped to the periscope pedestal on the port side and waited for the scope to breach the ocean's surface. Chris Coe took up station on the starboard side of the conn in front of the Number 1 scope from where he could watch the OOD and keep the sonar and Perivis displays directly ahead of him.

The periscope stopped its ascent and Richard Wickham bent his right eye to the viewing lens, first angling the search-scope lens to the sky, searching for the telltale signs of an approaching aircraft. Satisfied the sky was clear, he then duck-walked a full circle to carefully survey the Chinese coast.

"Six seconds," the periscope assistant had a stopwatch around his neck counting the time the periscope remained above the surface. "Seven seconds... eight seconds, sir..."

Wickham brought up the handles and stepped back from the scope. "Lowering Number Two scope."

The scope assistant rotated the Number Two scope lifting ring clockwise. "Lowering scope Two." The periscope slid back into the well.

"OOD, let's secure from modified battle stations and get back down deep," Coe's voice was a fraud of calm composure. Richard Wickham had lingered at the scope for longer than was good practice. Coe hoped the peril had been worth it.

"Aye, sir," the OOD nodded and then went on, "Secure from general quarters. Diving officer, make your depth three-two-five feet, all ahead slow. COW, lower all masts and antennas. All stations, conn going deep. Quartermaster sounding?"

"Sounding, aye, sir," the quartermaster went to the secure fathometer and took a sounding. The entire process lasted less than a heartbeat. "Sounding four hundred fathoms."

"Very well," the OOD confirmed.

"Sonar, aye."

"Radio, aye."

"ESM, aye."

The Chief of the Watch turned to the Captain. "Sir, all masts and antennas indicate down."

"Very well, Chief of the Watch. All stations, conn, securing the open Mic."

Coe strode to the forward bulkhead with Richard Wickham at his elbow. The XO rewound the footage the periscope had recorded, then queued the data to run.

The small monitor showed the lens of the periscope breaking the surface, the view of a lightening dawn sky and then a dark hulking mass on the horizon that stretched for miles, much of the landmass obscured by a thick dark blanket of pollution haze.

"Qingdao Harbor," Chris Coe said, like a surgeon diagnosing something fatal, inoperable and eminently malignant to a stricken patient.

In the twilight the horizon was lit with thousands of pinpricks of light, sweeping north and south, following the natural contours of the jutting coastline. Here and there on the high ground of promontories and headlands building structures could be identified, and there were small lights moving across the screen in the distance; most likely Chinese inshore patrol boats or perhaps tugboats making their way across the black expanse of the harbor. To the south, the high-powered periscope's lens had detected what might have been a mast on the horizon, close to the shore, bearing two-zero-five. The footage lasted just several seconds but Coe paused and froze frames for closer analysis, so that the two men stood in quiet consultation for several minutes. Wickham speculated the mast to the south might have been from an approaching Chinese destroyer or frigate heading towards the harbor entrance. Finally, the OOD's voice broke the somber spell.

"Sir, the ship is at three-two-five feet, all ahead one third."

"Very good," Coe said absently. His mind was distracted by what he had seen – and *hadn't* seen on the periscope's recorded replay. He wrestled for a long moment in silence, weighing the odds of taking further action; balancing the increased risk against the potential rewards. Finally, he decided to roll the dice one more time.

"COB take us back up to PD for a high look." It was a risk; normally the sub's periscope would be raised one or two feet above the ocean's surface, but a 'high look' would mean raising the periscope five full feet above the waves, significantly increasing the threat of visual or radar detection. It would also put the boat perilously close to the surface and in danger of broaching.

"Aye, sir."

The cautious, patient procedure to raise the submarine back to periscope depth began again.

"Standby for a high look, Scope 2," Coe announced.

"DOOW ready," the Diving Officer of the Watch reported.

"FC ready."

"DOOW, make your depth fifty feet." As each new order was given and immediately responded to the tension in the conn increased incrementally. Everyone in the control room understood the peril of the procedure. The strain showed on men's faces and in their jerking, tense movements and gestures. Everyone seemed to suddenly freeze, as though remaining motionless might help the boat stay undetected.

The *OKC* rose slowly, her massive steel hull beginning to sway slightly as she came under the influence of the surface swell. Once the boat was at the ordered depth and holding, the DOOW reported, his voice thick with strain, "Sir, at fifty feet."

Coe stepped up to the Number Two scope and focused the high-powered lens on the Chinese coastline. The day was beginning to lighten, the headland in the distance filling with definition and detail, bathed in the golden glow of the new morning. He lingered at the eyepiece for six long seconds then raised the handles and stepped back. "Lower scope 2. DOOW, make your depth one-five-zero feet."

"Sounding four-hundred fathoms," the quartermaster spoke.

"Very well, quartermaster. Good backup."

OKC submerged, eager for the safety of deeper water, while Coe strode to the playback monitor again. The XO rewound the brief snatch of footage and the two men pored over the imagery.

"A lot of commercial shipping," the XO grunted. In the brightening dawn light and with the view from the periscope at a higher elevation, both men could clearly make out the silhouettes of several commercial cargo ships clustered in the outer harbor. There were also three container ships anchored in the waters to the south of Qingdao, apparently waiting their turn to be escorted in to the port by a harbor pilot and tugs.

"That might be a warship mast," Richard Wickham went on, pointing to a dark outline of a ship deeper inside the mouth of the port, close to the southernmost headland.

Coe grunted noncommittally and looked up from the monitor. "OOD, all stop," he ordered. "Maintain our depth. I think we're close enough to shore. It's time to sit and wait and see if sonar can tell us what the Chinese are up to." By maintaining periscope depth rather than seeking the refuge of the bottom of the ocean, the boat would maintain VISINT and SIGINT intelligence. If Coe submerged to deep water, ascending again in such a difficult enemy environment might prove dangerous.

Oklahoma City slowed to a stop in the ocean and began to gently drift, a dark hole in the water. The boat was in its element; a lethal strike weapon, silent and deadly, and unexpected...

Around the ship the silence became almost eerie – until the sudden startled voice of the Sonar Sup crackled through the 21MC speaker above Coe's head at the conn.

"Conn, sonar! Multiple surface ships. Repeat multiple surface ships bearing two-seven-zero, two-seven-three, diesel engines. Too many to designate at this time." The Supervisor in the sonar shack had barely gotten the words out when the speaker blared to life again. "Conn, sonar. The TB-29 array just picked up a new contact, designated Sierra Three-one, bearing two-five-five. It sounds like an aircraft... no, it's a helicopter, sir. I can detect a high turbine rpm. It's heading our way, flying low!"

*

For three pounding heartbeats, Chris Coe froze and his mind became a turmoil of sick uncertainty and then alarm.

Had the Chinese somehow detected *Oklahoma City* and immediately scrambled warships and helicopters from Qingdao to launch an attack? Had the enemy somehow sighted the submarine's periscope when he had taken her up for the high look? Or were the Chinese simply making a random sweep of the waters beyond the busy harbor as a precaution against American submarine incursions?

Coe stole a glance around the control room and felt the eyes of every man upon him, their faces fraught with strain. For long seconds the silence and inertia stretched out. Coe understood this was a test of nerve. His inclination was to caution, necessitating him to hastily scurry away from the approaching Chinese flotilla surging out of Qingdao. But to do so might also be seen as an act of cowardice by the crew – and maybe it would be. Yet his fear that somehow *Oklahoma City* had been detected by the Chinese almost compelled him to panic.

Almost.

It was a coincidence; Coe clenched his sweaty palms into fists. It had to be. His faith in the stealth of his submarine was absolute. This was a Chinese operation being run as a routine mission to sanitize the waters off the harbor. But there was one way to be sure. He had to call the enemy's bluff and, in the process, gamble every man's life on his gut instinct.

"COB, lower all masts and antennas! Battle stations," Coe ordered and the DC lights around the submarine flashed three times, calling the entire crew to action.

"OOD, make our course due north," through the sheer force of his will he commanded his voice to calmness, "and make turns for eight knots. Diving officer make our depth eight hundred feet, thirty-degree down bubble."

"Aye, sir!" the orders were repeated with the crispness of men who had been waiting agonizing seconds for direction. The helmsman, diving officer and planesman all fastened their seatbelts as men around the control room reached for the nearest handhold to keep their balance.

"Attention in control," Coe announced, his casual tone masking his rising alarm, "We have approaching surface ship contacts bearing two-seven-zero, two-seven-three and a helo bearing two-five-five converging on our approximate position. I intend to move the boat to the north at slow speed to discern whether the contacts are in active pursuit, or whether we have stumbled into an enemy routine sanitizing operation. Carry on."

By turning north and going deep, Coe's change of course would decide once and for all whether the Chinese warships and ASW helicopter had detected him.

Oklahoma City slowly made speed, turning and diving deep at the same time. After five tense minutes, Coe strode into the sonar shack. *OKC* had moved three miles north of the harbor entrance, still seven nautical miles off the coast in deep water.

"Tell me what's happening with that helo," the Captain demanded.

"Sierra Three-one, sir. It's an old Harbin Z-9, licensed from the French. Designating Master Fifteen. I detected and classified at periscope depth just before we dived."

"Bearing?"

"Unchanged, sir. Still two-five-five."

Coe allowed himself a sly grin and a secret breath of relief. The Chinese helicopter would fly south of them by as much as four nautical miles if it maintained its current bearing. "Any sign of active sonar pinging?"

"No, sir," the Sonar Sup said.

"And the warships? What are we up against?"

"Still scrambled and confused, Captain. But there's at least one and probably two old *Sovremennys*. I'm designating Master Thirteen and Master Fourteen. I'm pretty sure there is a frigate in the mix too, but I can't yet identify." The operator traced his finger down the monitor at his work station, indicating the distinctive waterfall displays of the two Chinese destroyers being detected by the submarine's sensitive acoustic sensors.

"Bearing?"

"Unchanged, sir. Still bearing two-seven-zero and two-seven-three. They're doing turns for twenty-two knots and accelerating."

"Range?" Coe snapped.

"Eighteen thousand yards, sir."

"Any sign they're altering course to close on us?"

"No, sir. They're still surging and still maintaining their current course."

Coe leaned through the sonar shack door. "Officer of the Deck, ahead two thirds."

"Aye, sir," the OOD snapped. "Increasing my speed to ahead two thirds."

The helmsman at his station selected the 'two-thirds' position on the engine order telegraph and rotated the selector. A moment later the helmsman confirmed, "Sir, Maneuvering answers two-thirds."

In the background the Diving Officer continued to intone the *OKC's* depth, until the boat reached eight hundred feet.

A sonar operator suddenly leaned forward, his face a rapt mask of concentration, and clamped his hands over his headphones. He stayed like that, utterly unmoving for a heartbeat, his face tinted green by the reflection from the monitor in front of him. Finally, the man straightened and turned. "Z-9 Master Fifteen has gone into a hover, sir."

"Where?"

"Six thousand yards to the southwest."

Coe thought fast. Six thousand yards was a good distance away, but was it far enough if the enemy pilot began dipping its short-ranged sonar?

Most ASW helicopters around the world operated a sonar ball tethered to the end of a long winch-operated cable aboard the helo that could be 'dipped' into the ocean. If the sonar operator aboard the Chinese helicopter detected no foreign sounds from passive dipping, he had the option of going active; hammering the water in search for an acoustic return. If the sensors detected an enemy submarine, helicopter-borne torpedoes could be launched.

"Chief of the Boat, all stop!"

"All stop, aye, sir."

"OOD, have maneuvering spin the shaft as necessary," Coe finished.

"Aye, sir," the Officer of the Deck acknowledged, then turned to the COW. "Chief of the Watch to maneuvering, spin the shaft as necessary."

Oklahoma City was a nuclear-powered boat which meant it generated steam that was supplied to the boat's large turbines connected to a set of reduction gears, and then through to a very long shaft to which was attached the propeller. Once the valves supplying steam to the turbines were shut off, there was a danger the turbines could heat unevenly causing a bow or bend in the turbine rotors, resulting in catastrophic damage to the turbine blades. The solution aboard a nuc boat like *OKC* was to slowly spin the shaft a few times, even at 'all stop'.

The *Oklahoma City's* sophisticated propeller slowed. The hull around them creaked quietly and then an eerie silence wrapped itself around the boat. *Now all we can do is wait*, Coe resolved. *The next move is up to the Chinese.*

Chapter 6:

The submariners at their stations cast their eyes ominously upwards as if they might hear the approaching Chinese surface ships and the clatter of the enemy helicopter as it raced towards them. Coe stood rigid at the conn, wrestling to control his emotions; locked in his own internal struggle to remain outwardly poised and composed… and slowly losing the fight. He sensed the rising tension in the men gathered about him and a feeling of claustrophobia gripped him. Not knowing whether the *OKC* had been detected had left him paralyzed and no longer in control. He was tormented by sudden helplessness, forced to wait until the Chinese declared their intentions.

Coe stole a sideways glance at Richard Wickham and noted, with silent irritation, that the XO alone remained focused and apparently untouched by the approaching peril. His features were composed, his brow furrowed in concentration, yet his demeanor was calm and confident. In that moment Chris Coe resented the man for his disciplined courage.

"Damn him!" Coe thought in a flash of bitter envy. The XO had nothing more to do than obey orders, with no other responsibility than to execute them to the extent of his ability.

"XO, you have the conn," Coe snapped, more harshly than was warranted.

Wickham, who had been oblivious to the Captain's scrutiny looked up from the chart he was studying in abject confusion. "Aye, sir. The XO has the conn. The OOD retains the deck."

Coe stormed into the sonar shack. "Sup, what the hell is going on above us?"

The Sonar Supervisor pointed at the sonar control consoles. To the layman it looked like a handful of spaghetti had been flung across the screens. The entire display was awash with a confusion of contacts. The Supervisor jabbed his finger at a display. "A lot of these contacts closer to the harbor are fishing boats and small commercial ships," the man explained. "This is most likely a warship, approaching Qingdao from the south. It's following the coast, bearing unchanged and making fifteen knots," Coe recalled the distant mast he had seen through the periscope. "A couple of these are probably tugboats and pilot boats, moving out of the harbor – but they're not closing on our position. Best guess is they're preparing to bring in the queue of container ships waiting off the coast."

"What about the destroyers and the helo?" Coe was impatient.

"We've got a make on the frigate. It's a Type 054A 'Jiangkal II'. It's making turns for twenty knots, bearing two-six-eight," he pointed to the waterfall display to isolate the bright while line of the Chinese ship. "Designated Master Sixteen." Even as Coe watched, the line became brighter and began to bend, indicating an increase of speed and a slight course change.

"Range?"

"Five thousand yards, sir, but gradually opening. And these are the two *Sovremennys:* Master Thirteen, Master Fourteen. They about nine thousand yards to our south and turning further away, now bearing one-nine-five." The Supervisor expanded the time scale on the display to make for easier interpretation but it remained too complex for Coe to follow. He had to trust the experience of his operators to interpret the confusing scramble of data.

"What about Master Fifteen?" Coe felt the first glimmer of relief. His best interpretation was that the three Chinese surface ships were running some kind of choreographed search pattern across the waters beyond the harbor, criss-crossing an area of ocean five miles wide off the coastline. The two *Sovremennys* were working the waters around the queue of waiting container ships. The Jiangkal II was still a possible threat. It was passing to the south of *OKC*, but if it suddenly turned north…

"The helo is here," the Supervisor indicated the position of the Chinese Z-9. "It's now fifteen thousand yards south west of our current position."

"Active sonar dipping?"

"Aye, sir. He seems to be randomly moving around a square of ocean, hovering for a few minutes at each point to dip and actively ping, then moving to another point. He's not searching for us – he's searching for anything unusual. The last high-frequency dip was two minutes ago, bearing one-eight-five."

"Okay," Coe let out a breath and felt the tension in his shoulder relax just a little. He had been right after all; the Chinese had not detected *OKC*; they were sanitizing the waters off Qingdao. And if they did it once, they would most likely do it again. It was useful intelligence he would share with the *Minnesota* and *Colorado* before they arrived on station and the three submarines prepared for their attack on the departing arms convoy.

*

The wardroom's coffee tasted like battery acid, but Coe drank dutifully, using the distraction to keep him from the control room for a few minutes longer; fighting back the instinctive compulsion to closely oversee every moment of *OKC's* time on station. He was worn down by the relentless tension, running on adrenaline. He sat and fretted and fidgeted until the door opened and Richard Wickham appeared.

The XO poured himself a mug of coffee and sat at the opposite end of the table, so the two men faced each other. Coe glared. Wickham looked uncomfortable but resolved.

"Something you want to ask, XO?" Coe spoke quietly.

"Yes, sir," Wickham set aside his mug and drew a deep breath. "I wanted to know if you have a problem with my abilities or the way I am executing my duties?"

Coe arched his eyebrows, not surprised at the question, but surprised the XO had summoned the courage to ask him directly.

"No," Chris Coe said. "You're competent and efficient. My most recent evaluation of your performance reflected those opinions."

"Very well," Wickham nodded. "But I feel you should know that the Chief of the Boat has passed on to me his concerns about the growing resentment of the crew to the way you've been treating them… and I want to formally add my agreement to the verdict of the COB. I think you're driving the men too hard; expecting too much of them without acknowledging their efforts. They're good men, highly skilled and they're in a difficult environment. They could do with a little praise once in a while. So could the officers, sir."

"You think I'm too hard on you, XO?"

"I think you're too hard on everyone aboard the boat, sir," Wickham sidestepped the direct question. "And right now, the last thing these men need is to be distracted by a disconnect between the boat's two senior officers. It's not good for morale, and it's not good for the efficient running of the ship."

"So, you *do* think I'm being too hard on you personally?" Coe continued to probe.

"Captain, I don't think you trust me," the XO blurted.

"Do you disagree with the way I am executing our mission, or the decisions I have made since we entered the Yellow Sea?" Coe kept his face impassive and his eyes hard.

"No, sir. You're the skipper and you make all the calls, and my job is to execute your orders. But it's also my job to advise and offer forceful backup in times of crisis. The fact is that you're not using me, or my ability. You're leaving me out of the command loop, and the crew have noticed. It erodes my credibility with the men."

Chris Coe set down his coffee cup and pushed it aside. He narrowed his eyes to hide a sudden flare of temper – resenting the XO's tone

"Do you think I've done anything contrary to the requirements of the mission or to unnecessarily jeopardise the safety of the boat, Mister?"

Wickham flinched. The use of the word 'mister' had altered the nature of the conversation and the XO became instantly alert and guarded. The air in the room crackled with sudden ominous tension.

"No, sir."

"Good. Then this is all about your hurt feelings, and if there's one thing I cannot abide, it's bitter whining. I'm not here to 'validate your personhood', XO. This isn't a school playground for the politically correct; it's a battlefield in the middle of a war zone," despite himself, Coe's frayed temper simmered to the boil and spilled over. His voice rose and he spoke through clenched teeth. "So I suggest you either man up and do what the mission requires of you, or relieve yourself of duty. It's your choice, but don't – ever – come to me again whining about having your precious feelings hurt. I don't have time to pander to your ego when the lives of every man aboard this boat are at stake. Are we clear?"

Wickham's face suffused with a hot flush of color and his mouth pinched into a bitter pale line. He was seething. "Crystal clear, sir."

*

For seventy-two tense hours, the *Oklahoma City* lay off Qingdao Harbour in deep water, altering her position every few hours but always remaining more than seven nautical miles off shore, rising only briefly every twelve hours to 'clear the broadcast' for signal traffic before plunging back down into the depths. Four more times the Chinese Navy ran sanitising operations off the port entrance, repeating their criss-cross search pattern while *OKC* remained passive and silent... and undetected.

It was a challenging time for the crew and officers aboard the submarine; endless hours of taut boredom followed by anxious spells of alarm as a flotilla of enemy destroyers and helos swarmed from the harbour like ants from a disturbed nest, hammering the waters off the coast with active sonar.

Chris Coe's relentless obsessive energy drove him on; compelled him to oversee every minute detail aboard the boat until his features became drawn and his pallor ashen with the strain and fatigue. He slept only fitfully, prowling the passageways in the quiet hours, restless and brooding, until, finally, it was time to move the boat east to the agreed rendezvous point to join up with the arriving submarines that would complete the attack force.

The details of the rendezvous had been meticulously coordinated prior to *OKC's* departure from Guam. Coe spent fifteen minutes in his cabin reviewing the instructions and almost fell asleep hunched over the laptop containing the Top-Secret orders. He snapped himself awake, aware that exhaustion was overwhelming him, and lurched to the head to splash cold water on his face. His reflection in the small mirror was haggard, his eyes underscored by deep smudges that were the color of old bruises. He headed to the wardroom for coffee.

Coe finally stepped into the conn, still with the steaming mug clenched in his hand, and nodded curtly to the XO who had been operating as the ship's Command Duty Officer in Coe's absence.

"Anything I've missed?" Coe was surly and irritable.

"No, sir."

"Very well. The CDO watch is secured. It's time to move into position to meet up with *Minnesota* and *Colorado*, Mister Wickham."

"Aye, sir," the XO kept his eyes on the overhead displays lest Coe see the simmering resentment in his eyes. The relationship between the two senior officers aboard had deteriorated significantly since their confrontation in the wardroom. Now the two men barely bothered to maintain a professional degree of civility. The frosty exchange was noticed by the men in the control room.

"OOD, make our course zero-eight-eight, all ahead one third," Coe gave the order.

The rendezvous location was a point east of Dagong Island, with *OKC* ordered to remain above three hundred feet and the arriving submarines to remain below four hundred feet, giving enough depth separation between each boat for safety.

Once in position, *Oklahoma City* shut down her engines and remained alert on battle stations until a sonar operator suddenly announced, "Conn, sonar. I'm picking up faint machinery noise, approaching slowly on bearing one-eight-five."

"Bearing steady?"

"Aye, sir."

Coe confirmed *OKC's* location and re-checked the time. As a precaution, Richard Wickham ordered the fire control tracking party to begin working on a torpedo solution for the new contact.

"Captain, a call on the UQC," a petty officer's voice broke the tension.

Coe strode to the Gertrude, picked up the phone receiver and thumbed the Transmit button. "Bravo."

After a heartbeat of hissing distorted delay, a voice replied, "Alpha."

Coe allowed himself a moment to let out a long silent breath of relief, as did the rest of the men crowded into the control room. He depressed the Transmit button again, some of the tension already drained from his voice now the approaching submarine had identified itself. "Alpha, this is Bravo. Stand by for a range check."

"This is Alpha standing by," Coe heard the reply. The voice over the underwater telephone was distorted by the ocean between the submarines, sounding metallic and hissing with echo.

"Bravo, this is Alpha. Range check follows. Five... four... three... two... one. Mark!"

Richard Wickham and two petty officers in the control room all started their stopwatches simultaneously, then listened intently for the response from the arriving submarine.

"Snap!" the voice over the Gertrude was sharp and crisp in Coe's ear.

"Mark!"

The XO made the calculations in his head, factoring the delay time between responses against the average speed of sound through water to calculate the range. A young officer at the 'secondary plot' table located behind the conn confirmed Wickham's maths.

"Range to *Minnesota* is just over four thousand yards, sir."

"Very well," Coe grunted. *Colorado* would probably be further astern of the *Minnesota*, he guessed – maybe another two thousand yards to the south.

"Bravo, this is Alpha, my Mike Tango Tango Four Zero."

"Alpha. Roger. My Mike Tango Tango thirty-eight assuming Corpen one-eight-zero, Sierra four," the two submarines exchanged ranging results and navigation details.

Around the control room the officers and men at their battle stations all visibly began to relax. They had been operating alone in a difficult enemy environment for several days. It was a relief to finally have support, and to know that they weren't entirely isolated.

*

The *Minnesota* and *Colorado* were both *Virginia*-class (SSN-774 class) nuclear-powered fast-attack submarines, designed for a broad range of open-sea warfare missions. They were the latest generation of American sophistication, ultimately designed to replace aging *Los Angeles*-class boats like the *Oklahoma City*. They were huge hulking monsters of the deep, costing more than 2.5 billion dollars each. But for all their technology and sleek electronic sophistication, Coe did not envy the commanders of the *Minnesota* or *Colorado*. A traditionalist to the core, Chris Coe was perfectly happy commanding a 'real' submarine – not some high-tech gadget dreamed up and designed by committees of technology-fascinated bureaucrats.

Coe pressed the transmit button on the Gertrude. "Arnie, welcome to China," he spoke slowly, to give the transmission through the water every chance at clarity. "It's good to have your company. I assume Stephen is with you?" Coe addressed the commander of USS *Minnesota*, Arnold Gainsborough, in the casual manner of old acquaintances – which they were.

"Hiya, Chris," Arnold Gainsborough's voice came clearly through the receiver. "Yes, Stephen is here too, but I'm afraid the party has been delayed which means a change of plans."

"Delayed?" Coe frowned.

"Latest Intel from SUBPAC suggests the departure of our friends has been put back by four days. It's a long time to be waiting around in a demanding environment, so you're being ordered to take your boat south towards Ningbo to raise some hell and keep our friends looking the other way. Stephen and I will keep a watch in case our friends try to sneak out the front door early."

Coe thought quickly. He was both relieved and anxious. Waiting four more gruelling days for the Chinese arms convoy to depart Qingdao would have taxed his patience and physical reserves to the limit – but to operate as a lone wolf against Chinese shipping targets was an intensely demanding challenge he had not anticipated or prepared himself for.

"Roger all," Coe said. Ningbo was a major Chinese trading port six hundred nautical miles to the south, nestled on the foreshore of Hangzhou Bay. It was also the Fleet Headquarters for the Chinese East Sea Fleet and the home port of up to half-a-dozen destroyers, a handful of frigates, several corvettes, and a number of Chinese diesel-electric submarines. They were leaving the frying pan and steaming headlong and alone into a huge fire.

"Official orders for the tasking will be put on the broadcast. When they're ready, you'll be alerted by an SUS charge," Arnold Gainsborough said.

"That's good news," Coe feigned eagerness. In truth he was still unsure how he felt about the altered conditions of the mission, but pride would not let him display anything other than relish at the prospect of unrestricted warfare against the enemy's warships and merchant fleet – despite his misgivings.

"Good hunting, Chris. I have to say, I envy you. I'd trade places with you in a heartbeat for a chance to plunder. Seems like you're having all the luck."

Coe ended the transmission and turned to the control room, still in a fog of numb ambivalence. "Officer of the Deck, secure from battle stations. OOD make our depth six-four-zero. Navigation, I want a course and SOA set for the Port of Ningbo – asap. Get the Nav up here immediately."

*

For a split second the operator in the sonar shack was unsure what he was seeing on his screen.

"Conn, sonar. Explosions in the water."

Within seconds Coe and the XO were at the operator's side, staring at the irregular waterfall pattern being displayed.

"What have you got, McGrath?"

The operator indicated the bright green lines spilling down the monitor's screen, then typed a series of commands. "Sir, we've got three separate explosions, the detonations spaced regularly at two second intervals."

"Range?" Chris Coe asked.

"Unknown sir. But not close."

"An engagement?" XO Mark Wickham puzzled.

"I don't think so, sir," the sonarman swung around in his seat. "In fact, I think it's the SUS signal we've been expecting."

Chris Coe called to the submarine's radio operator. "Radio, report any VLF signal."

"VLF negative, sir."

"Very well."

Up until 2004, US submarines sailing deep in the world's oceans could be contacted with urgent messages by extremely-low frequency (ELF) signals originating from installations established in the Chequamegon National Forest near Clam Lake, Wisconsin, or a twin facility in the Escanaba River state forest near Republic in Michigan. Both installations had been abandoned due to rising costs and local environmental backlash.

Since that time the navy had used a VLF system with varying degrees of success. The VLF signal worked on the same principals as ELF but with less reliability and less penetration in deep water.

Occasionally the navy resorted to using SUS charges. The Signal, Underwater Sound explosive charges were more commonly used for marine seismic research. Consisting of a small amount of TNT, the SUS charges could be exploded in a sequence from a T-AGOS ship; one of the Navy's Ocean surveillance vessels normally used to gather acoustical data from across the world's oceans. The US ships were operated by civilian contractors for the Military Sealift Command. Two ships from the fleet's *Victorious*-class of vessels regularly worked the waters of the Pacific.

Coe made his decision. "We're going up to PD."

USS *Oklahoma City* rose cautiously towards the surface, corkscrewing slowly in the depths to allow her sonar to search the surrounding ocean for threats as she ascended. At a depth of one hundred and fifty feet, and with her baffles cleared, each contact held by solution had a solution generated on it in the submarine's sophisticated fire control system. The process took several tense silent seconds. Finally, the Officer of the Deck spoke in a voice suppressed by strain.

"Captain, the ship is at one-five-zero feet. All ahead one third and on course one-eight-zero. I have cleared baffles and hold three sonar contacts all classified as merchants, all outside of thirty thousand yards. Request permission to go to PD and clear the broadcast."

"Proceed to periscope depth and clear the broadcast," Captain Coe gruffed.

The submarine rose to a depth of sixty feet. Coe waited until the boat leveled and he heard the OOD make his report.

"No close contacts."

"No threat contacts," ESM reported. "Request permission to raise the ESM mast."

"Chief of the Watch, raise the ESM mast," the OOD confirmed.

Chris Coe stepped forward. "Let me take a look, LT."

He bent his brow to the Type 18 periscope and swept the sky for threats first, then scanned the ocean's horizon in every direction through the high-powered 16x magnification. The XO watched the control room monitor that repeated a television image of everything the Captain was seeing through the periscope.

The sky was clear, the ocean relatively calm.

"Okay," Coe muttered without peeling his gaze away from the periscope's viewing port.

The *Oklahoma City's* 21MC circuit hissed to life and an operator in the radio room requested number BRA 34 to query the broadcast. The request was echoed immediately by the OOD. "Chief of the Watch, raise Number One BRA 34. Radio room, query the satellite for the broadcast."

The RMOW (Radioman of the Watch) keyed out the boat's call sign on the UHF satellite broadcast band to receive any incoming messages. The digital screens began to light up with a single page of coded orders. The RMOW relayed the message to the server destined for the conn display and the CO's stateroom. Captain Coe ordered the OOD to man the scope.

Everyone in the control room went very still and silent.

TOP SECRET LIMDUS (RELEASABLE TO AUS/UK)
FROM: CINCPACFLT
TO: USS OKLAHOMA CITY
INFO: COMSUBPAC (00/01/N3/N33)

COMSUBLANT (00/01/N3/N33)
COMSEVENTHFLT (N00/N3)
COMSUBGRU SEVEN (NOO/01/N3/3A)
TASKFORCE GAMMA.
SUBJECT: EXECUTION OF CINCPACFLT OPORD 2000.1E.
1. CINCPACFLT 2000.1E ENCLOSURE ONE TAB A IS IN EFFECT.
2. TASKING UNRESTRICTED SUBMARINE WARFARE ON ALL PRC FLAGGED VESSELS IN VICINITY OF NINGBO, CHINA.
3. PROCEED TO 29DEGN1 121W5 MHN 60x20x20 nm4. DEPTH ZONE SURFACE to 500FT6. SOA SPEED 24KTS2.
4. YOUR OPERATING AREA IAW REFERENCE A IS ESTABLISHED. INTERCEPT AND ENGAGE ALL ENEMY TARGETS OF OPPORTUNITY.
5. REPORT CONTACT PRIOR ATTACK.

MHN was a submariner's water management abbreviation for a 'moving haven' – a four-dimensional box which moved with the vessel at a pre-determined speed as the boat raced towards its destination. The box was orientated twenty miles each side of a track designed to avoid collisions in peace time, and inadvertent friendly fire during war from other US assets converging on the same point in the ocean. By training, submariners never intentionally left their assigned water management track for fear of courting an avoidable disaster that could easily ruin a career. The box moved with a designated SOA (speed-of-advance) and provided an 'ahead' distance and a 'behind' distance. These strict movement controls would allow COMSUBGROUP SEVEN to maintain a sophisticated program to ensure no other allied submarines interfered with the boat's transit south.

Captain Coe read the message; his expression carefully controlled. He was acutely aware that every man in the submarine's control room was watching him, yet he said nothing for long moments until he finally turned on his heel to address Richard Wickham.

"XO, I want the officers assembled in the wardroom in fifteen minutes."

*

Oklahoma City's officers were seated and silent when Chris Coe strode into the wardroom. He wasted no time and did not sit. Instead, he stood at the head of the table while the officers watched him, attentive as school students, with flip-top notebooks in their hands.

"We've been tasked with attacking enemy shipping around the Port of Ningbo," Coe explained. "Our mission has been changed because the convoy due to leave Qingdao that we were sent to destroy has been delayed by several days, according to latest intelligence. We got this job because we're faster than the two *Virginias*, and our weapons load is more suited to the mission."

He looked around the room. The officers were already tense and strained from the relentless pressure of warfare. He noted the grim expressions on their faces at this daunting new challenge. They would be alone in hostile waters, and once they launched their attacks, they would be relentlessly hunted and constantly in danger.

The pale expressions around the room irritated Coe. The SSN culture was to fight alone. The boats were designed for that purpose and the crews trained in that self-reliant manner. Coe understood the culture but clearly his young wardroom did not. His eyes turned malevolent, and his voice cracked across the silence like a whip. "When we get on station and find ourselves alone, unsupported and outnumbered – we are in the right place. This is the job, people, and it's what we do. Suck it up."

The biting tone of his voice cut across the room. A couple of the younger officers flushed, shame-faced. Coe stayed silent for a full thirty seconds, making no effort to conceal his icy contempt.

"Nav, I want you to plot an SOA to take us south of Ningbo, but I want to stay in deep water and avoid enemy warships until we are in position. We will not attack any shipping north of the target. I want nothing to allude to the possibility that other US submarines are off the enemy coast – so we get into position *south* of Ningbo and we only attack enemy targets heading south out of the port."

The boat's Navigator nodded.

"Weps, I want every torpedo and Harpoon we have aboard tested and checked before we reach our attack point. If something's faulty, I want it stripped down. Once we're in the thick of the enemy's shipping, I don't want any munition wasted. Am I clear?"

The Weapons Officer scratched notes in his pad and nodded. "Aye, sir."

"Engineering, I want any routine maintenance work completed within the next twenty-four hours. If there's a problem with any machinery, I want you to report it to me personally."

"Aye, sir."

"Gentlemen, the waters off Ningbo are heavily populated with dozens of islands, both large and small – that will give us good water to hide and evade in. But the port is also the Headquarters of the entire Chinese Navy's East Sea Fleet. It will be heavily defended and bristling with enemy air and surface assets. I will make an announcement to the crew about our new tasking and then it's up to all of you to keep your teams alert and ready for action at a moment's notice. Any questions, or comments?"

No one spoke. The officers sat somber and chastened.

"Dismissed."

Chapter 7:

For almost thirty hours, *Oklahoma City* ran south at over twenty knots until she lay fifteen miles off the eastern tip of Zhujiajian Island in the Putuo Sea. Coe studied the plot with the Nav at his shoulder and pointed to a cluster of small islands and atolls that lay further to the south.

"Here," he described a small patch of ocean with his finger, sixty nautical miles to the southwest amongst a cluster of small Chinese islands dominated by Jiushan Chain Island. The location would place the American submarine fifteen miles due east of Baisha Bay and well within striking distance of coastal shipping routes.

The Nav re-plotted the course and the Assistant Navigator, the XO and finally Chris Coe concurred. The *Oklahoma City* crept further south with four hundred feet of ocean above them, moving more cautiously now that they were approaching fleets of small commercial fishing craft.

Captain Coe stepped over to the Navigation Plot and stood beside the Officer of the Deck. His expression became a frown of thoughtful contemplation. The submarine's track showed *Oklahoma City* running southwest and passing to the north of Maluan Island.

Captain Coe prowled the conn for several minutes, moving about the confined space like a haunting ghost. Finally, he came back to the Officer of the Deck.

"OOD, let's slow her down for thirty minutes." As he spoke, Coe re-checked the time. In half an hour the Midwatch would be on. "I want to put the thin line out."

"Aye, sir," the OOD answered, then raised his voice and barked instructions. "All ahead one third and make turns for seven knots. Man stations to deploy the TB-23."

The order was echoed several times.

"COW, inform maneuvering that we are deploying the TB-23," the OOD added.

After running at high speed for so long, the sudden diminished hum of the submarine's reactor coolant pumps being set to 'slow', and the muted sounds of the propeller made the conn seem eerily quiet. The crew felt the 688 shuffle in the ocean as she decreased speed.

Coe waited until the towed-array was deployed, paid out from a receiver in the port horizontal stabilizer. The TB-23 Thin Line Towed Array was a sophisticated acoustic detector, with a hydrophone array over nine hundred feet long, towed on a two-thousand-foot length of cable. The TB-23 was specifically designed to detect very low frequency noise at very long ranges.

After just a few minutes, the sonar supervisor clamped his hands over his headphones and then leaned forward to closely study the glowing screen in front of him.

"Conn, sonar. I'm picking up a faint contact."

The Executive Officer was the first man to reach the sonar station. Richard Wickham studied the display for several seconds, then turned to Coe.

"It appears to be a Chinese flotilla or convoy, Captain," Wickham said, pointing to a wide arc of broadband towed array contact on the screen bearing zero-four-two or three-one-eight. "It's a cluster of ships, probably five or six at a guess, travelling south."

Because the towed array's 'beams' were conical-shaped cones emanating from each hydrophone along the TB-23, broad band and narrow band contacts registered on each side of the array. The ambiguity required the submarine to speed up, turn, then slow again until the array re-stabilized and the source of the contact could be further defined.

"Range?"

"It's a wild guess, but probably something more than a hundred thousand yards, sir. I think they're still a couple of convergence zones away at least."

The sonar supervisor discreetly caught Chris Coe's eye. "Sir, my best guess is that it's the second CZ. It's got to be something more than fifty nautical miles for sure. We're picking up the contact on the spherical array, but it's intermittent. It comes in loud and clear, then disappears."

Sound normally passed through water in waves that were typically predictable, but there were some areas of deep ocean in which the sound waves bent toward the surface and then often bounced back into the sea, eventually to be turned upward again by pressure. These areas of anomaly were labelled convergence zones. A CZ could allow sonar to detect sound waves at far greater ranges than normally possible. In deep water these zones frequently occurred at intervals of about thirty miles.

At such long range, the conical bearing of the towed array was little more than an approximation. Distance degraded acoustic signal definition. The Chinese convoy could be many miles further to the left or right than the monitor indicated.

"Okay," Chris Coe sighed like a man about to embark on a long and arduous journey, "we'll try to get a sharper picture of exactly what we are dealing with. XO, take us east and we will see if we can resolve ambiguity and drive the bearing rate to make sure they really are out there and still a ways off. I doubt we'll lose contact, and if we do, it will only be temporary. They're making so much noise they won't be hard to locate again. If we can confirm the bearing, we'll send off a contact report."

The art of submarine warfare demanded patience and nerve. Coe made a display of casual indifference as *Oklahoma City* turned silently to the east, heading back out into deeper water. A sense of new urgency filled the control room and Coe let the tension wash over him, apparently unaffected. Behind his eyes his mind was wrestling with the gymnastics of the tactical situation. *If* the contact firmed and proved to be a substantial Chinese military convoy steaming south from out of the East China Sea, where would be the best place to lay in wait? And would the enemy ships pass to seaward of Jiushan Chain Island, or alter course and suddenly dash towards the shelter of Chinese shore-based air cover?

His only tactical option was to move northeast and intercept the convoy before it reached the islands, launching his attack from well out to sea. His decision made, he strode back into the sonar shack.

"Did we get what we needed?" he barked.

"Yes, sir," the sonar supervisor nodded, not turning away from his panel. "I have resolved the ambiguity. Regained Sierra Three-Two, bearing zero-four-five. They are to the northeast. Can't drive the bearing much – they are out there."

"The contact is coming from further out to sea?" Coe intuitively distrusted the report. "Why aren't they following the coastal shipping route?"

"It could be an enemy ploy," the XO guessed. "Maybe it's a military convoy and they're using an alternative ocean route to transit south as a precaution against coastal attacks."

Chris Coe grunted and stared intently at the display for a long moment before speaking again. He could feel a sudden lift in his own heart-rate – his instincts coming alert to the thrill of the hunt.

"Good," Coe took a long last glance at the broad spoke of noise on the screen. "XO, get it plotted and have a contact report prepared. Then give me a course to intercept."

*

"How do you want to play this, sir?"

The XO and Chris Coe were standing at the plot table while the navigator added the latest information to the picture they were rapidly compiling on the composition of the Chinese convoy.

The contact with the enemy ships had grown steadily stronger as the minutes passed, and *Oklahoma City's* sonar operators had already classified a Type 071 *Yuzhao*-class amphibious transport. The ships screw-blade count revealed a speed of eighteen knots. They had also singled out at least one Type 052C *Luyang II*-class destroyer and two, possibly three, Type 903A *Fuchi II*-class Naval replenishment ships. The Chinese seemed to have a screen of small escort ships ahead of their transports. The closest contact was thirty-three miles northeast.

Coe straightened and glanced around the *Oklahoma City's* attack center. Everyone was focused, working with calm purpose. He went to the conn and addressed the men at their stations.

"Attention in the Attack center. We are tracking a convoy of Chinese ships including warships and transports. I intend to drive east off their track which is currently south-southwest, then come to PD and shoot at the heavies, and then the transports. Sonar – remain alert for any submerged contacts," Coe announced. "Any questions or comments?"

The men of the submarine's Tracking Party remained silent.

Coe nodded. "Carry on."

"Aye, aye."

"OOD, keep our speed steady at eight knots. If we need to change our angle of attack, I want to do it slowly and early."

"Aye, sir."

"XO, man battle stations. And I want to reload two of our tubes with Harpoons," Chris Coe made the last-minute decision.

"Sir?" Wickham blanched. "What about ASW? The Chinese are bound to –"

"Two ADCAPs will have to be enough, XO," Coe kept his tone neutral. "We'll have to take our chances with any Chinese destroyers shepherding the convoy. Our priority is the *Yuzhao*-class amphibious transport and any other troop carrier or military cargo ship in the convoy. The Harpoons have to be the priority."

"Aye, sir," the XO nodded curtly. There was a flush of chastened color on his cheeks, but he barked the order.

"Torpedo room," the XO called from the conn. "Back haul torpedoes from tubes two and four and reload tubes two and four with Harpoons."

The response came back immediately. "Back haul tubes two and four and reload tubes two and four with Harpoons. Torpedo room aye, sir."

Oklahoma City's full torpedo room complement for the mission was twenty-six weapons, including four loaded in the torpedo tubes. The mission loadout was a mix of Mk 48 ADCAP torpedoes and Harpoon anti-ship missiles.

Coe knew he could fire his Harpoons at the Chinese right now. But without first identifying specific targets his missiles could be wasted on a frigate. He was after bigger prizes.

The Mk 48 ADCAP torpedoes were the submarine's stock-in-trade weapon. With a top speed of over fifty knots and a range well over thirty-thousand yards, the Mk 48 ADCAP was lethal. The weapon could be used against surface targets and submarines; a wire-guided torpedo that took targeting data during the initial stages of the launch from the BSY-1 fire control system aboard the submarine. Only during the final stages of an attack would the ADCAP use its active seeker to home in on its objective.

"Torpedo Room reports that tubes two and four have been back hauled and reloaded with Harpoons," the Weps voice cut across the Captain's quiet thoughts.

Coe took one final glance at the plot and went forward to sonar. One of the sonarmen was hunched forward at his station, his face a mask of deep concentration, his features painted green by the glow from the screen in front of him.

Coe watched the man silently until his spell of focus seemed to break with a wry smile of triumph.

"You got something, son?" Coe gruffed.

"Aye, sir," the sonarman sat back so the skipper could see the screen at his station clearly and pointed to the display. "I think I've got a bearing on a Chinese Type 075 *Yushen*-class landing helicopter dock. I just identified a cluster of low-frequency sonar pings and some compressed cavitation. I'm still trying to isolate the engine signature."

"Stay on it. Let me know when you have something concrete."

The *Yushen*-class Type 075 was a major vessel in the PLAN flotilla. The amphibious assault ship measured almost eight hundred feet long, displaced over thirty-thousand tonnes and carried a wartime cargo of thirty attack helicopters. The Chinese had plans for three of the massive assault ships but to date only the *Hainan* had been launched and commissioned into active service.

It took another thirty long minutes before the discovery could finally be classified.

"Conn, sonar. Chinese Type 075 assault ship, bearing zero-eight-eight, speed eighteen. Designate Master Twenty-Six. We've also identified an old Chinese Type 056 corvette on bearing zero-eight-four, Designate Master Twenty-Seven."

"Conn, aye. Range to the heavy?"

"Estimate thirty-five miles, sir." The BSY-1 computers calculated the approximate distance, but the actual precise range was insignificant. What really mattered was that the bearing was accurate. As long as the target was within reach of the Harpoons, they would hit.

Coe made a mental list of the individual Chinese ships that had been identified and classified. To the best of sonar's reckoning the enemy convoy comprised a destroyer and a corvette performing escort duty for a Type 075 assault ship, a Type 071 amphibious transport and two twenty-five-thousand tonne replenishment ships. It was a handsome prize and a worthy target of opportunity that *OKC* might have missed entirely but for the powerful sensors of its towed array.

"XO, I think we'll send these bastards a message," Coe said grimly. "If we can get some licks in early, we can even the numbers before it turns into a fistfight."

Richard Wickham said nothing.

The submarine-launched Harpoon variant was called the UGM-84. It was essentially a standard missile wrapped within a buoyant capsule shaped to fit inside a torpedo tube. Once launched, the capsule rose to the surface, discarded the capsule's nose, and ignited its rocket booster. Once the booster had performed its task, it too fell away leaving the Harpoon's turbojet engine to carry the missile the rest of the distance to its target, guided by its radar seeker.

"Take us up to PD, speed four knots," Chris Coe instructed the OOD. He waited patiently, his expression impassive while the submarine came shallow, as always observing a carefully rehearsed set of procedures and precautions. The OOD's face was tight with concentration.

"We are at periscope depth," the OOD said at last, releasing the breath he hadn't realized had been wedged in his throat. "No close contacts."

"Very well," Coe acknowledged. "Firing point procedure, Master Twenty-Six, with a single Harpoon."

"Ship ready, speed and depth verified, sir," the OOD said crisply.

"Solution ready," the XO said.

"Echo Master Twenty-Six, bearing zero-eight-eight," ESM declared.

"Weapons ready," Weps said. Each new voice seemed to ratchet up the tension.

"Shoot on generated bearings, Harpoon, Master Twenty-Six!"

"Standby. Shoot!" Weps voice filled the Attack center.

The deck beneath Chris Coe's feet seemed to vibrate, and a deep thunder-like rumble trembled through the submarine. For a long moment there was just eerie silence and a vague sense of anti-climax.

The OOD at the submarine's periscope announced, "Capsale broach, missile transition to cruise!"

"Normal launch," Weps confirmed. "Harpoon is on its way."

"Post launch tube 2 and reload with an ADCAP Mk 48!"

*

With the first Harpoon streaking out across the sky behind a billowing tail of grey smoke, Coe barked at sonar, "Bearing to Type 071 *Yuzhao*-class amphibious transport, Master Twenty-Four?"

"Conn, sonar. Master Twenty-Four, Type 071 *Yuzhao*-class bearing zero-eight-four, range thirty-six miles. Speed eighteen knots."

"Very well," Coe growled, caught up suddenly in the blood-lust of combat. "Firing point procedure, Master Twenty-Four, tube four with a single Harpoon."

"Ship ready, speed and depth verified, sir," the OOD reported.

"Solution ready," Richard Wickham confirmed.

"Weapons ready," Weps said.

"Match final bearing and shoot!"

"Standby. Shoot!" Weps' voice was loud with his own tension.

Again, the *Oklahoma City* shuddered as the second Harpoon missile roared from its launch tube and broke the ocean's surface in a wild roar of noise and billowing exhaust smoke.

"Post launch tube 4 with an ADCAP!"

With the two Harpoons unleashed and streaking northeast towards their Chinese targets, Coe ordered the *Oklahoma City* to dive.

"Aye, sir," the OOD nodded. "Diving officer, make your depth five-two-five feet, all ahead one third. COW, lower all masts and antennas. All stations, conn going deep. Quartermaster sounding?"

"Sounding six hundred fathoms."

"Very well," the OOD confirmed.

"Sonar, aye."

"Radio, aye."

"ESM, aye."

The Chief of the Watch turned to the Captain. "Sir, all masts and antennas indicate down."

"Very well. Make our course zero-six-zero to intercept the Chinese convoy, all ahead full."

"Aye, sir," the round of repeat backs rattled around the control room, finishing with the helmsman who acknowledged the Diving Officer's order. *Oklahoma City* sank down into the depths at a fifteen-degree dive, turning more northerly and accelerating at the same time.

On the surface, more than a dozen Chinese powerful land-based and sea-based sensor systems immediately detected the launch of the two Harpoons. The warships in the convoy too became almost instantly alert. The orderly spaced line of ships broke apart in pandemonium, each vessel making a dramatic course alteration and accelerating as the inbound Harpoons dashed towards them. The sea around the Chinese ships became a confusion of white-water wake as the Type 075 and Type 071 turned to port and the accompanying cargo ships turned starboard. The Chinese destroyer and corvette both accelerated, the corvette shadowing the Type 075, firing off clouds of chaff in an attempt to decoy the incoming danger away from the convoy's flagship.

The first Harpoon reached the Chinese flotilla just six minutes after launch and began its final descent. Too late, the Type 075 fired its HQ-10 SAM system defenses and when those missiles failed to intercept the incoming danger, the two H/PJ-11 30mm CIWS began tracking the incoming Harpoon's trajectory and opened fire, throwing up a curtain of steel around the vessel as a last-ditch defense.

The Harpoon slammed into the huge assault ship's forward deck, missing the vital bridge superstructure but tearing a massive hole in the hull and destroying several helicopters before ripping through the ship's lower decks, causing catastrophic damage. The Chinese vessel disappeared in a fireball of flames and smoke for tense long seconds and when it re-emerged through the haze it was listing to port and wallowing heavily in the water, still streaming a towering column of black oily smoke as the ship's officers tried to turn her into the wind and keep the ship afloat.

"Conn, sonar! Explosion on the surface, bearing zero-eight-eight. The first Harpoon has hit Master Twenty-Six."

Coe reached the sonar shack in three long, urgent strides. "Any secondary explosions? Any sounds of breaking-up noises?"

"Getting some small secondary explosions now, sir," the sonar operator had his hands cupped over the headphones he wore as though he might hear more clearly. "But they're not ship-killers. Maybe stores or supplies blowing up somewhere inside the hull. But she's still afloat. Speed..." he paused, "maybe six knots, bearing now two-seven-zero. She's making a lot of noise."

Coe was disappointed but not surprised. He had never really expected a single Harpoon to sink the Type 075; the chances of such cataclysmic damage were minimal, especially if the Chinese ship had managed to secure all her water-tight compartments before impact. But he had landed a heavy punch. Now it was time to close for the kill.

The second Harpoon struck Master Twenty-Four, the Type 071 *Yuzhao*-class amphibious transport dock, sixty seconds later. The Chinese ship was not as large as the Type 075, but nor was it as nimble as a corvette or a destroyer. Despite its desperate attempts at evasion there was no escape. Once the inbound Harpoon was detected off the port bow, the ship's forward AK-630 30mm CIWS system locked on and began tracking. The Captain of the ship ordered a sharp turn to starboard to allow two more of the onboard CIWSs to track, then ordered the chaff launchers into operation. When the Harpoon was within range, the CIWS systems erupted, their six-barreled 30mm rotary cannons disappearing behind a wall of white smoke and a thunderous hammering roar of fire.

The Harpoon's five hundred pound high-explosive warhead slammed into the amphib's superstructure and detonated on impact, destroying the bridge, and killing every officer in the command center.

"New explosion, bearing zero-eight-four!" the sonar operator aboard *Oklahoma City* seemed to jump with a start as the second Harpoon smashed into the amphibious transport dock's superstructure. "Range thirty-four miles. Secondary explosions... Sir, the Type 071 Master Twenty-Four has been hit."

Coe acknowledged the report with grim satisfaction. A ragged cheer erupted around the control room as the crew at their stations celebrated. Coe, however, knew the work was far from finished. He strode back to the conn and ordered the Nav to plot a course to intercept the stricken Type 075. Richard Wickham overheard the order and blanched.

"Sir?" he voiced his concern in a discreet hush to Coe to avoid being overheard. "Is that a wise decision? We still have a Chinese destroyer out there and it's going to be hunting us. In another thirty minutes these waters will be swarming with Chinese ASW aircraft and any nearby warship, all looking for revenge. Maybe we should consider evading – clear datum and look for other opportunities."

Chris Coe's features burned with sudden outrage. He drew the XO aside and thrust his face close to the other man, his words hissed with seething contempt. "Mister Wickham, there are only two types of enemy warships: floating and sunk. Need I remind you that this submarine carries no weapons of limited response. Our mission is to shoot the sons-of-bitches and then hunt them relentlessly until they're on the bottom of the ocean, and that's exactly what I intend to do. Get in the god-damned fight or get off my boat!"

*

For fifteen minutes the *Oklahoma City* surged northwards in deep water on a course to intercept the stricken Type 075 Chinese landing helicopter dock. As the submarine closed the distance, the tactical picture in *OKC's* attack center filled in quickly.

The two damaged Chinese warships were holding a course due east, most likely making for the nearest port, limping for safety at slow speed. Around them were gathered the two Type 903A *Fuchi II*-class Naval replenishment ships and the corvette, positioned a mile to the south and sailing a parallel course.

Eight miles further south, and located between the *OKC* and the convoy, the Type 052C *Luyang II*-class destroyer was actively pinging the ocean with its helicopter aloft to the southeast, dipping its sonar array.

"Attention in Control," Coe went to the conn and addressed the men around him. "Our Harpoon missiles have successfully hit and damaged the two Chinese heavies. They are currently sailing east towards safety in company with the rest of the Chinese convoy. We're not going to let them get away. It is my intention to close on the enemy vessels, evading the Chinese destroyer currently seventeen miles ahead of us, and then to fire torpedoes at the two damaged Chinese warships. If time and the tactical situation permits, we will then attack the two naval replenishment ships. Are there any questions?"

Around the control room the men at their stations remained mute. "Very well," Coe snapped. "Carry on."

He strode stiffly from the control room and made for his stateroom. Once inside he splashed cold water over his face, fighting off a crushing sense of fatigue and nausea. When he looked in the small mirror, his reflection seemed somehow eroded; as though the unrelenting strain of the mission had sandblasted his features, leaving them craggy and misshapen.

A sudden polite but firm knock at his cabin door jolted him from his thoughts.

"Come," Coe toweled his face dry.

Richard Wickham stood in the threshold of the doorway, his mouth working in agitation, his cheeks flushed. In his eyes was a look of indignation.

"You got something to say, XO?" Coe's voice was confrontational and a direct challenge, almost testing the young XO's resolve.

"Yes, sir."

"Fine," Coe threw down the towel but did not sit. The two men stood face-to-face in the tiny cabin space like boxers in the ring before a fight. "Speak your mind."

"Sir, I feel duty-bound to tell you that if you continue to pursue the stricken convoy of Chinese warships to our north, we run the very grave risk of not being able to reach our rendezvous with the *Minnesota* and *Colorado* should the Chinese arms convoy depart Qingdao unexpectedly."

"I am aware of the risk," Coe said flatly.

"Sir, this entire mission is governed by our orders – and our orders were to attack the arms shipment and prevent the Chinese from supplying the Pakistani Government with war materiel that might encourage them to join the Axis Alliance…"

Chris Coe held up his finger, and so deeply-ingrained was Richard Wickham's training that he instantly faltered into blustering silence. Chris Coe smiled thinly but there was no trace of humor in the gesture. His eyes were cold, his expression savage.

"XO, our orders *guide* our actions. A commander of a US attack submarine is *governed* by his fighting instincts. We are a man of war, Mister, *and we are at war!* This isn't a simulation. It isn't an exercise. This boat was built to sink enemy shipping and I intend to see it perform its role to the best of its ability and at every opportunity presented. It seems to me that you're more focussed on covering your ass and dotting every 'i' and crossing every 't' than you are with killing the enemy."

"Sir…"

"That might be fine practice in theory, but in the real world, when real torpedoes are firing, men's lives are at stake…" Coe spoke brusquely across Wickham's attempt to interrupt him, his voice rising and his temper flaring until the words from his mouth were spat with whiplashing contempt, "… *all your theory becomes bullshit and all that matters is sinking the enemy!*"

The tiny cabin space crackled with tension. Richard Wickham's lips moved. His face was pale, and the words came out hoarse and whispery. "Very well. Then at least we should report to CINCPACFLT."

"Fine," Coe said, his temper still simmering in his eyes. "Send your message, XO. But make it quick. As soon as we close on the Chinese destroyer, there will be no more opportunities to make radio contact with anyone until after those enemy heavies are wreckage on the ocean floor."

Chapter 8:

When Chris Coe returned to the conn, *Oklahoma City* was ten miles south of the Chinese destroyer and closing, still in deep water, well below the thermal layer. The destroyer was making a lot of noise, sprinting, and then drifting across the ocean, running a gridded search pattern, while the ship's helicopter darted from one site to the next with its dipping sonar like a bee buzzing between a garden bed of flowers.

Coe stood at the plot table in the aft of the control room for a full sixty seconds studying the display until he felt confident he understood the rhythm of the Chinese destroyer's search pattern. When sonar reported the destroyer suddenly sprinting further east, Coe quickly stepped up to the conn.

"Chief of the Watch, to the three-inch launcher space. Have the primary and secondary launchers loaded with ADCs set in noise mode. Set the primary device with a five-minute time delay and the secondary launcher device a ten-minute time delay. Also in control standby to launch the ADC Mk3 from the CSA launcher programmed to run in echo repeat mode." The launchers were located on the port side of the ship allowing Coe to baffle the launcher air noise from the destroyer with his own ship, muffling the sounds of them ejecting from the boat.

"Aye, sir," the COB said, though by the sound of his voice he was clearly puzzled.

"The moment we launch, I want a course change west to two-seven-zero, speed eight knots."

"Aye, sir," COB repeated and then set about passing along orders that would have crewmen altering the time delay controls for the countermeasures.

The process took several frantic minutes before the broadband and echo repeater countermeasures were loaded and prepared for operation. Coe kept an eye on the course of the Chinese destroyer and the movements of the hovering helicopter, guided by a constant stream of reports from the sonar shack. The helo was moving away to the northeast now, preparing to dip its sonar back into the ocean.

"Rig ship for ultra-quiet."

In deep water and at speeds below ten knots, *OKC* was almost immune to active sonar detection, yet Coe continued to err on the side of caution, creeping through the depths, stealthy as a thief.

When the Chief of the Boat reported all was in readiness, Coe took a deep breath – and paused. The stunt he was about to pull was unconventional and unorthodox. It didn't come from any naval training manual, instead the tactic had been refined on attack center simulations. Now he would put his tactical hunch to the ultimate test, gambling with the ultimate stake; his men's lives.

"OOD, shoot primary launcher!" Coe ordered.

The orders were repeated. A moment later there was the sound of a loud *'bang'* and hiss of air venting off from inside the ship.

"OOD, shoot secondary launcher!"

The orders were again repeated.

"Control, launch one CSA launcher!"

The men at their control panels were all on standby, anticipating the order. On Coe's command the broadband and echo repeaters were jettisoned into the ocean. They burst from their launch tubes and hovered in the deep water, dormant until their timers silently ticked down the remaining seconds until activation.

"COB, turn left two-seven-five, speed twenty knots!"

"Aye, sir! Turning left two-seven-five, speed twenty knots," the COB repeated and then relayed the order. The helmsmen, too, were anticipating the change of course. *OKC* turned in the ocean and steadied smoothly on her new bearing. It was critical to Coe's plan that he began opening datum as quickly as possible. At twenty knots, *OKC* would travel about three-thousand yards in the five minutes before the countermeasures activated. Even if the Chinese responded instantly, and even if they were able to immediately pinpoint the source of the noisemakers, a Chinese torpedo launched from the helicopter could only detect up to a thousand yards.

When the submarine's countermeasures suddenly activated in the ocean exactly five minutes later, the Chinese destroyer reacted, dashing towards the source of the underwater disturbance. The ship's helo flew low over the site three times, dropping a cluster of sonar buoys into the ocean, and then hovering to launch its torpedo.

By the time the Chinese had reached the location of the *OKC's* noisemakers and received permission to initiate their attack, *Oklahoma City* was more than two miles to the east and Coe let out the long breath of relief he had been secretly choking on. He realized, with a self-conscious start, that he had been standing statue-like with his hands clenched into tensed fists.

"Fire control, bearing to the Chinese convoy ships?"

"Bearing three-five-five, sir."

"Range?"

"Nineteen miles."

"Very well. Officer of the Deck make your course three-five-five. Increase speed to twenty-five knots."

Again, *Oklahoma City* turned smoothly in the ocean, and began accelerating quickly towards her hapless prey.

"Attention in the attack center. We are now inside the enemy destroyer and are closing on the Chinese convoy. Fire control, our priorities are the Type 075 and the Type 071. I need firing solutions on both targets for Mk 48 torpedoes." Around the control room Coe sensed a change of atmosphere; the tension turning to exhilaration as the submarine stalked its targets. "It is my intention to continue on our present course for a further nine minutes before slowing to fire our weapons at the enemy."

*

"Man battle stations torpedo," Chris Coe's voice cut through the quiet tension that had blanketed itself over the control room. Richard Wickham, in his role as the fire control coordinator, relayed the order to the ship's torpedo room over the sound-powered phones. Coe wanted the torpedo tubes armed and ready well before they reached his intended attack position. It wasn't a conventional tactic; usually a submarine commander would wait until the boat had slowed before opening the outer doors.

"Torpedo room, fire control. Make tubes one and two ready in all respects, including opening the outer doors," Wickham relayed the instruction.

The torpedo room acknowledged the order and completed the evolution in quick time, then reported back. Wickham reported to Coe, "Captain, tubes one and two are ready in all respects. The outer doors are open."

"Very well, fire control," Coe acknowledged without turning. He was concentrating fiercely, making complex mental calculations, and visualising his attack. In his mind he saw the two Chinese heavies, separated by about a mile of water, both stricken warships streaming black columns of smoke as their crews fought desperately to control the onboard fires and keep the vessels afloat. Screening the ships would be the two freighters and the corvette. Time was critical. He needed to launch his strike and clear datum before the surrounding ocean was swarming with inbound Chinese shore-based ASW aircraft.

Coe's plan was to fire torpedoes simultaneously at both the Chinese heavies and then close to finish off the two escorting freighters. He explained his plan to the control room, and as the *OKC* closed to within fifteen thousand yards of the ragged convoy, Richard Wickham announced, "Captain we have firing solutions on both Master Twenty-Four, the *Yuzhao*-class amphib, and Master Twenty-Six, the *Yushen*-class Helicopter assault ship."

"Very well," Coe acknowledged. "Helm ahead one third. Maneuvering make turns for six knots."

OKC began to slow in the ocean until she was creeping through the depths.

"Fire point procedures, Master Twenty-Six tube one and Master Twenty-Four tube two. Single Mark 48 ADCAP torpedoes."

"Aye, sir!" the order was repeated.

"Master Twenty-Six bearing three-five-zero, speed six knots, range twelve thousand yards. Master Twenty-Four bearing three-five-three, speed six knots. Range twelve thousand yards," the FCC reported. "Solutions ready!"

"Ship ready!" the Officer of the Deck echoed.

"Weapons ready!" Weps confirmed.

Coe nodded and made a final mental check. They were seven miles south of the convoy – within easy range of the Mk 48s. Once the Chinese convoy was destroyed his plan was to clear datum to the east, heading back out into deep water, eluding the Chinese ASW aircraft that must be, even at this moment, closing quickly.

"Sonar, conn, stand by."

"Conn, sonar, standing by."

Chris Coe paused for one more heartbeat and then gave the orders to launch the attack. Once again he noticed that in the heat of battle, his exhaustion sloughed away and the shroud of fatigue that made his bones ache and his movements stiff lifted. He felt alive; in his element now that the long fraught hours of tension were behind him and all he had to do was obey his warrior instincts.

"Match sonar bearings and shoot tube one!"

"Match sonar bearings and shoot tube one, aye!"

The submarine seemed to pulse in the ocean as the first Mk 48 whooshed from its torpedo tube. The CSO's voice sounded hoarse with the tension. "Tube one fired electrically! Impulse return, normal launch, good wire."

"Match sonar bearings and shoot tube two!"

"Match sonar bearings and shoot tube two, aye!"

Again, the *OKC* shuddered in the water as the massive torpedo was thrust from its launch tube.

"Tube two fired electrically," the Combat Systems Officer confirmed the second successful launch. "Impulse return, normal launch, good wire."

The two Mk 48s completed their wire-clearance maneuvers, running at high speed directly for their separate targets.

Coe let out an adrenaline-loaded sigh of satisfaction. "Time to enable?"

Once launched both Mk 48s rose to their search depths, following guidance from a complex onboard algorithm. Once at its enabling point, each torpedo would go active and begin searching for targets, commencing the detecting and homing sequence of the torpedo's path. The enabling point was a critical moment because it also signified the instant that enemy ships might detect the incoming torpedo and begin evasive maneuvers.

"Four minutes, ten seconds, Captain."

"Very well."

The control room remained eerily silent while the minutes counted down. Weps kept a constant monitor of each weapon's mode-messages which were being sent back from the torpedoes as they raced towards the convoy.

Finally, a Combat System Operator declared, "First weapon, detect! detect! Homing, bearing three-five-zero, speed seven knots, range ten thousand yards. Weapon is going shallow."

"Matches solution for Master Twenty-Six," the Fire Control Coordinator confirmed.

A moment later the CSO reported torpedo two had detected and was homing. It was the report Coe had been waiting anxiously for.

"Weps! Cut the wires. Reload tube one and tube two!"

"Aye, sir," Weps responded from fire control. "Reload tube one and tube two."

The OOD ordered a three-degree down angle to ensure the wires left the ship cleanly while in the background Coe heard the orders being repeated to the torpedo room, but his focus was on the track of the torpedoes. One corner of his mind was counting off the seconds while around him the control room remained a tense hive of activity.

"Conn, sonar. The first weapon has acquired Master Twenty-Six, the Type 075. Torpedo increasing speed."

"Sonar, aye. Is the target turning or altering speed?"

"No, sir," the sonar operator's voice seemed strangely calm despite the drama of the moment. "Still bearing three-five-zero, still making six knots."

Coe grunted. Most likely the stricken assault ship had been so badly damaged by the Harpoon strike that it was unable to take evasive action. Coe imagined the officers and crew aboard the Chinese ship, aware that their death was imminent but helpless to do anything about the fatal blow. He felt no sympathy – only a cruel primal surge of savage triumph.

"Conn, sonar. The second weapon has acquired Master Twenty-Four, the Type 071, bearing three-five-three."

"Sonar, aye. Fire control, time to impact both torpedoes?"

"One minute thirty seconds, sir," Richard Wickham had a stopwatch in his hand, trailing from a thin blue cord slung around his neck. Coe didn't need the answer; he already knew it. He had made the mental calculations minutes earlier and there were detailed displays around the conn that provided a picture of the contacts, the torpedoes and their cones of search. On these displays the times, ranges and impact predictions were already being presented.

"Very well. Fire control I need firing solutions for the two Type 903A *Fuchi II*-class Naval replenishment ships, Master Twenty-Eight and Master Twenty-Nine."

"Aye, sir," Richard Wickham responded.

Coming up with firing solutions for the two vessels took several minutes. Both of the Type 903As were turning south and accelerating, putting space between themselves and the heavies and presenting their bows to further incoming torpedoes in a last-ditch attempt to avoid destruction.

Coe chaffed against his impatience as the fire control team struggled with the TMA (target motion analysis) solutions, gritting his teeth, his jaw clenched. He could hear the pounding pulse of his own blood at his temples, and for a brief moment all his senses seemed heightened so that every voice around him sounded clearly, and the scents of sweat and raw anxiety filled his nostrils. Time seemed to slow, so that every second became clearly imprinted on his consciousness. He heard his own strained breathing and then the voice of a sonar supervisor came loudly through the speaker above the conn.

"Conn, sonar! Surface explosion, bearing three-five-zero. Master Twenty-Six, the Type 075 took a direct hit. Torpedo one has impacted."

"Sonar, aye," Coe forced his voice to a monotone. "Give me an update on the surface picture."

"Conn, sonar. Master Twenty-Six is dead in the water, sir. I'm hearing breaking up sounds. Master Twenty-Four is just beginning a slow turn to the south…" It figured, Coe thought. The commander of the Type 071 was trying to turn his crippled ship towards the incoming torpedo in the vain hope that the ship's more narrowed bow profile might save his vessel from destruction. "Master Twenty-Seven and Master Twenty-Nine, the two Type 903As, have both made turns to the south and are accelerating," sonar concluded the report.

"Sonar, aye," Coe said and turned to glare at Richard Wickham. "XO, I need those firing solutions!"

"I have the solutions, sir."

"Very well. Fire point procedures, a salvo, Master Twenty-Seven tube three and Master Twenty-Nine tube four. Single Mark 48 ADCAP torpedoes."

"Aye, sir!"

FCC reported, "Solutions ready!"

"Ship ready!" the Officer of the Deck confirmed.

"Weapons ready!" Weps said.

"Match sonar bearings and shoot tube three Master Twenty-Seven. Shoot tube four Master Twenty-Nine."

"Match sonar bearings and shoot tube three Master Twenty-Seven and tube four Master Twenty-Nine, aye, sir!"

Coe braced his balance as the two torpedoes leaped from their tubes and a shudder washed through *Oklahoma City*.

No sooner had Coe given the order than a cry from sonar cut across the frantic action around the control room.

"Conn, sonar. Surface explosion, bearing three-five-three. Master Twenty-Four has taken a direct hit. Torpedo two has impacted. She's sinking sir. I can hear flooding."

Another cheer went up around the *OKCs* control room, but Coe did not even hear the noise. So deep was his concentration, so completely overloaded was his imagination visualizing the surface picture, that he was utterly oblivious to the ragged celebration. He needed to clear datum to the east quickly, but he also needed to be sure the Chinese convoy was completely destroyed.

He cast a quick glance around the control room; every man was hunched over a monitor or frowning with intense concentration at their station, and he grudgingly admitted that they had performed well throughout the attack. So far it had been a text-book operation…

"FCC, time to impact Master Twenty-Seven and Master Twenty-Nine?"

"Six minutes thirty seconds."

"Very well. Officer of the Deck, take us up to periscope depth."

"Aye, sir," the OOD's surprise put a split second of delay between the order being given and repeated.

"Attention in the attack center," Coe made the sudden announcement. "We have completed successful attacks against Masters Twenty-Four and Twenty-Six. I want to come right to PD to assess the damage and to press the attack if necessary. Any questions or comments?"

Oklahoma City came up from the depths turning a full circle to clear her baffles. As she came shallow, the voice of the Diving Officer counted off the ascent, "Passing two hundred and fifty … passing one-ninety…"

The OOD spoke next. "Captain the ship is at one-five-zero feet, speed four. The FCC holds no contacts inside five thousand yards. Ready to go to periscope depth."

"Very well, proceed to periscope depth."

The *Oklahoma City* rose up from the ocean with only the Number Two scope raised. The moment the scope broke the surface the OOD said quickly, "No close contacts."

"Raise the ESM mast," the Officer of the Deck ordered.

"Raise the ESM, aye, sir," the order was echoed.

The board in front of the ESM operator lit up the instant the mast broke the surface. "Multiple threat contacts, sir!" the operator began calling out the radar names, bearings and signal strengths. The information began flowing to the FCC, so he could attempt to correlate, identify and locate.

"Very well," Coe remained unperturbed. He had expected nothing else. The Chinese would be in panic mode right now. The electronic atmosphere would be jammed with radio traffic. "Raise the scope."

Coe bent to the periscope as it rose out of the well and pressed his eye to the viewing lens even before it had completed its elevation. He turned the scope north and peered for three long seconds at the smoking fiery devastation on the skyline. The periscope assistant at his side began calling out the bearings. When Coe steadied on a contact he called, "Pictures!" as he thumbed the scope's high-speed camera button.

The Type 075 assault ship was just a dark smudge against the sky beneath and ugly black smear of oily smoke and flame. The ship appeared to be sinking stern first. Through the billowing clouds he could see the blackened hull, buckled and broken. He turned the scope slightly and the Type 071 came into view, about a mile further to the east. The ship was still afloat, but its back had been broken. The ship was listing heavily to port, part of its mangled superstructure hanging in the ocean. The ship was embroiled in black smoke and tongues of leaping flame. Then, as he watched, another explosion ripped the ship in half, and it began to turn turtle and sink.

Between the two stricken heavies, the two Type 903A naval replenishment ships were still afloat, both of them steaming south towards the *OKC* at speed, their snub bows surging white water about their hulls. Coe figured torpedo impact on both ships would be less than a minute away, but he couldn't linger on the scope to witness their destruction. Instead, he tilted the lens upward and scanned the sky to the east. A dark speck in the upper corner of the lens caught his eye, and he peered for two full seconds before the sickening realization struck him. A deafening high-pitched scream from a search radar filled the control room.

"Down scope!" Coe stepped back from the scope as though he had been electrocuted. The assistant pulled the orange ring to lower the periscope.

"Diving officer. Emergency deep!" Coe cried.

Automatically the crew around the control room exploded into action. *OKC* plunged her nose down at a fifteen-degree angle and began to dive. Once the boat reached one hundred and fifty feet, Coe ordered, "Helm ahead flank! Cavitate! Cavitate! Make your depth seven hundred feet, thirty-degree down! Enemy ASW aircraft bearing zero-eight-seven coming down on us."

Oklahoma City's great engines erupted into life as a terrifying white-ice of alarm gripped every man in the control room. Voices cried out, repeating the Captain's orders. Men lunged for handholds as the ship accelerated and dived, the planesman and helmsman grim-faced and infected with the sudden panic.

"Conn, sonar! Sonobuoys in the water, bearing zero-nine-zero."

"Left full rudder!" Coe barked the order.

"Left full rudder, aye!" the OOD repeated. *Oklahoma City* turned hard to the east.

"Sonar, any torpedoes in the water?"

"Negative, sir. We've just been overflown by a low-level aircraft, turboprop at a guess. He has passed to the west and is turning back for another sweep."

"Sonar, aye. OOD, make your course one-eight-zero."

"Aye, sir. Making my course one-eight-zero."

The agonizing seconds of tension ticked on as *OKC* continued to dive deep, her bow steeply declined. When the diving officer confirmed they were at seven hundred feet, Coe allowed himself a brief moment of respite. "OOD, ahead two-thirds. Hold steady course one-eight-zero."

"Aye, sir. Ahead two thirds, steadying course one-eight-zero."

In the sudden crisis, and with *OKC* making so much noise to evade and dive, Coe had no idea whether his two torpedoes had impacted Master Twenty-Seven and Twenty-Nine, but now that small issue didn't matter. He had far greater problems to deal with; he had planned to clear datum to the east and, once in deep water well away from the Chinese coast, had intended to move north to make the rendezvous off Qingdao with *Minnesota* and *Colorado*.

Now he had been cut off and driven south.

His triumphant attack had turned into a tactical nightmare.

*

For four more long hours, *Oklahoma City* continued to run south, remaining deep, her speed steady. Every moment took the submarine further away from Qingdao. Coe stood at the conn, shifting his weight from foot to foot in rising agitation. He wanted desperately to pace the control room like a caged lion but could not let his rising despair show to the men. He was desperately tired. He couldn't recall the last time he had slept uninterrupted for more than a few hours. The unrelenting nervous tension brought on by the strain of the mission had made it impossible for him to delegate operational details to Richard Wickham and his senior officers even though he was now paying the price for his obsessive micromanagement. Unrelenting anxiety would not allow him to rest and had abraded the edges of his patience so that every passing minute they steamed further south seemed to darken his temper further.

The control room was eerily silent, each man concentrating on his task but all of them affected by the Captain's brooding unrest until the despair seemed a physical thing that crushed down on them all. The somber pall was broken only by intermittent reports from sonar of Chinese ASW aircraft and helicopters in the vicinity.

For the first two hours of their flight south Coe had fretted that the Chinese were searching the ocean off the coastline relentlessly hunting for *Oklahoma City*, but as the reports continued to come from sonar, he gradually realised that the *OKC* was not being stalked; instead, the entire east coast of the mainland seemed alive with enemy ASW activity.

He went to the plot and studied the submarine's location, standing beside the Nav. *Oklahoma City* was passing south of Taizhou in deep water sixty nautical miles off the coast. Coe searched his memory and recalled everything he remembered about the Chinese port from the intelligence reports that had accompanied his mission orders.

The Port itself was not the home of a major Chinese naval presence, but in the past it had been an important harbor used by the Chinese for amphibious assault exercises and was regularly used by the Chinese as a fleet stop for destroyers and frigates that operated as part of the East Sea Fleet. In 2019 China's second aircraft carrier, *Shandong* had spent two months at Taizhou running a series of amphibious assault exercises in conjunction with fleet amphibs and destroyers.

Coe wondered for a moment whether the increased Chinese ASW presence was connected to increased naval operations around the port and then dismissed the conjecture as pointless. He had bigger, more pressing issues to deal with.

"We're approaching the southern boundary of our Ops Area, Captain," the Navigator sounded bleak. "If we maintain our course and speed, we're going to run into serious water management problems."

Water management for US submarines was a critically important issue, especially in times of war. Governed by Group SEVEN at Fleet Activities in Yokosuka, each active submarine was allocated an operations area and a water management scheme which translated to a box, an area of ocean or sometimes merely a corridor to transit through. Once an area was assigned to a submarine for engagements, any detected contact within the area could safely be assumed as hostile and engaged. US submarine commanders were trained never to violate their water management schemes. The entire system was designed to avoid tragic 'blue on blue' incidents and to clarify the status of contacts. If anything submerged was detected in a submarine's killing field, Coe could confidently engage and sink it with no classification required –and no questions asked.

Coe took one last despairing look at the plot, and then caught Richard Wickham's eye and summoned the XO to a quiet corner of the control room with a meaningful look.

"It's now impossible for us to return to Qingdao to meet up with *Minnesota* and *Colorado*," Coe finally conceded in a hushed voice that would not be overheard by others. "Continued Chinese ASW activity up and down the coast and the risk of long-range patrols make the possibility of speed run to the rendezvous an unacceptable risk. XO, I want you to prepare a message to notify Captain Gainsborough, aboard *Minnesota*, of our circumstances. Once he has acknowledged, we will send a follow-up message to CINCPACFLT notifying them of our position, what has happened, and requesting a follow-on tasking."

"Aye, sir," Wickham's face remained impassive, though inwardly he felt vindicated. He had warned Coe of the risks associated with driving home the attack against the Chinese convoy and had been proven right. It gave him grim satisfaction but no cause for celebration. *OKC* was isolated and alone on a hostile coast. The sense of their peril quashed any brief moment of gratification he might have felt.

With the order given, Coe returned to the conn. Sonar was tracking an approaching low-altitude Chinese turbo-prop ASW aircraft bearing two-eight-zero. If it maintained its current course, the aircraft would pass five miles astern of the submarine. It was one of three enemy patrol craft that had criss-crossed the waters off Taizhou Harbour in the past hour.

"Sonar, aye," Coe acknowledged the report. Now he had decided to message *Minnesota* and CINCPACFLT, there was no longer a need for haste until he received further instructions. "Officer of the Deck, make your speed ahead one third and make preparations to come to periscope depth."

*

Through a network of sophisticated intelligence sensors, the J-3 Joint Operations coordinators at CINCPACFLT and SUBPAC were keeping a careful monitor on *Oklahoma City's* shifting position and were supplying regular updates to Arnold Gainsborough aboard *Minnesota*. The two *Virginia*-class submarines had been ordered to remain at periscope depth continuously so that when Chris Coe contacted the two boats off Qingdao over the EHF SATCOM line, *Virginia's* commander responded almost immediately.

"OOD, raise the Number One BRA-34. Radio, get SUBPAC up on the EHF and request them to have *Minnesota's* Charlie Oscar come up on the net," Coe gave the orders crisply.

"Aye, sir," the orders were repeated back and a few moments later a voice from radio broke the tense silence.

"Conn, radio. *Minnesota's* Charlie Oscar on the net. Use the Number One red hand set."

Chris Coe picked up the receiver. "*Minnesota*, this is *OK City*, over."

"Roger, Chris. Read you Lima Charlie. Looks like you have been busy down there."

"Roger, Arnie. Very good hunting but we're unable to come north again to join you."

"Roger all. Understand. Continue."

"Am asking the boss for new follow-on tasking here for us and for the two of you."

"Understand all. Standing by. Good hunting. Out," Commander Gainsborough ended the call and his voice dropped off the line. Coe took a breath and then spoke directly to comms operators at CINCPACFLT.

"CINCPACFLT, this is *OK City* standing by this net for follow-on tasking."

"Roger OK City. We are working that out now with SUBPAC to give you new water and tasking to the south. It will be on the Broadcast at the top of the hour. CINCPACFLT out."

"Okay. *OK City*, out."

Coe ended the EHF SATCOM call and ordered the mast lowered. All radio transmissions from a submarine were potentially locatable from enemy national sensors and Coe felt instinctively vulnerable to detection in the aftermath of the brief transmission. He ordered the *OKC* to move ten miles to the west to clear datum.

No sooner had the Officer of the Deck reported the EHF antenna secured and had acknowledged the order for the submarine to turn west than a sudden call from sonar sounded a fresh alert.

"Conn, sonar. Significant sonar activity bearing one-nine-five!"

Coe made it to the sonar shack door in three long strides. "What have you got Sup?"

The Sonar Supervisor didn't need to explain. Coe could see it for himself on the sonar screens; a thick white spoke of broadband noise almost due south of *OKC*.

"Any idea of range?" Coe's eyes narrowed.

"Well over a hundred thousand yards, sir. It might be as far as three convergence zones. It's impossible to tell at the moment." Three full convergence zones might mean a distance as great as a hundred miles or more.

The thick white spoke represented a significant number of enemy ships all making noise. "What about screw or blade counts?"

"No, sir," the sonarman seated in front of the console shook his head. "All we're picking up at the moment is a cluster of noise that would suggest it's a major movement of enemy surface ships."

"Heading?"

The sonarman shrugged again. "Sorry, sir, it's just too early to tell. The acoustic signal is so vague, I'm not even sure of the exact bearing."

Coe nodded then put real urgency into his voice. "Son, you've got exactly one hour to find out everything you can about that contact, understand?"

"Aye, sir."

"In the meantime, let's turn this over to the Fire Control Party to start some TMA and I'll get the boat moved so we can drive the bearing rate."

Coe went back aft into Control and ordered the OOD to turn *Oklahoma City* to the east. "Make your course zero-nine-zero to get a leg at fifteen knots to see if you can drive the bearing rate on a new contact."

"Aye, sir," the order was acknowledged. *OKC* moved in the water, turning east and running silently. When Coe returned to the sonar shack, the atmosphere in the small space had turned electric.

"I've pinned it down, sir. Bearing confirmed at one-eight-seven. They're probably a hundred miles or more south of us, close to the Chinese coastline and moving southeast. I'm guessing ten surface ships, maybe more."

"Southeast? Are you sure of that, son?"

"It's an educated guess, sir… but I'd bet on it."

Coe hustled from the sonar shack and returned to the plot table in the aft section of control. He touched an area of ocean off the Chinese coastline where the enemy contact was estimated and stared hard at the Nav. "Sonar has picked up a significant number of enemy surface ships in this area," he indicated a square of ocean with his fingers. "And there's a good chance they're moving southeast..." his finger traced a line across the chart until it hit a landmass. "If sonar is right, it could represent part of a Chinese attack or an invasion fleet sailing towards Taiwan."

Coe summoned Richard Wickham and shared his assumption with the XO, his voice restrained but his tone urgent. "When we go up and get our new water assignment from CINCPACFLT at the top of the hour, I want an urgent message sent immediately to Group SEVEN and CINCPACFLT. Tell them a Chinese naval assault against Taiwan might be imminent and request instructions."

Coe was sure that Group SEVEN and CINCPACFLT would be monitoring the nets and expected that details of this new contact information would receive a rapid response. He ordered the ship's floating wire antenna deployed which would allow *OKC* to monitor the VLF broadcast continuously and then ordered the OOD to take the submarine back west towards the Chinese coastline at slow ahead.

"XO, while we're waiting for a response from PACFLT, I want this boat made ship-shape for immediate action. Reload all tubes and reposition rounds in the torpedo room for reloads. And I want the crew battle messed and rested. Make sure the section Chiefs are on top of urgent maintenance, starting with anything that needs fixing in fire control and the reactor. Am I clear, Mister?"

"As a bell, sir," Richard Wickham said stiffly. "I'll see to it right away."

Coe nodded and turned on his heel, headed to his stateroom. In the doorway to control he stopped suddenly. "Notify me as soon as we hear from Command. Once we have our new orders there will be a briefing for all officers in the wardroom."

Chapter 9:

The digital screens in front of the Radioman of the Watch aboard *Oklahoma City* began to light up with a single page of coded orders at the top of the hour. The RMOW relayed the message to the server destined for the conn display and the CO's stateroom. Chris Coe read the orders sitting at his desk, dizzy and nauseous with exhaustion.

TOP SECRET LIMDUS (RELEASABLE TO AUS/UK)
FROM: CINCPACFLT
TO: USS OKLAHOMA CITY
INFO: COMSUBPAC (00/01/N3/N33)
COMSUBLANT (00/01/N3/N33)
COMSEVENTHFLT (N00/N3)
COMSUBGRU SEVEN (NOO/01/N3/3A)
USINDOPACOM CAMP SMITH, HI (JOO, J3)
COMFLTFOR NORFOLK, VA (NOO, J3)
TASKFORCE GAMMA.
SUBJECT: EXECUTION OF CINCPACFLT OPORD 2000.1E.
1 CINCPACFLT 2000.1E ENCLOSURE ONE TAB A REMAINS IN EFFECT.
2 TASKING UNRESTRICTED SUBMARINE WARFARE ON ALL PRC FLAGGED VESSELS IN VICINITY OF NINGBO, CHINA.
3 PROCEED TO 29DEGN1 121W4 MHN 60x20x20 nm0. DEPTH ZONE SURFACE TO TEST DEPTH. SOA SPEED 24KTS6.
4 IAW REFERENCE A. YOUR HOME PLATE ONE IS ESTABLISHED. INTERCEPT AND ENGAGE ALL ENEMY TARGETS OF OPPORTUNITY.
5 PROVIDE A CONTACT REPORT PRIOR ATTACK.

Coe noted with an intrigued lift of his eyebrow that USINDOPACOM at Camp Smith, Hawaii, and COMFLTFOR at Norfolk had been added to the list of order notifications. USINDOPACOM was the joint commander of all forces in the Pacific, and Fleet Forces Command oversaw all naval forces for readiness in both the Atlantic and the Pacific. He came from his stateroom grimly resolved, his determination rising to the surface through dense layers of fatigue at the realisation there would be more dangerous work ahead. Like a boxer on the ropes, exhausted, he rallied himself one more time and put purpose into his stride and voice.

"XO," Coe found Richard Wickham at the conn. "There will be a meeting of all officers in the wardroom in ten minutes. See to the arrangements."

"Aye, sir."

"Officer of the Deck, make our course one-eight-seven and take us to flank speed. Diving Officer, make your depth four-four-zero feet."

"Aye, sir," the repeat backs echoed around control, the room suddenly infused with renewed purpose.

*

Chris Coe stood waiting in the wardroom as the *Oklahoma City's* officers filed silently into the room. Their expressions were grim, and the desultory conversation died on the men's lips at the doorway when they saw Coe awaiting their arrival. Richard Wickham was the last to enter the room. He shut the door behind him and took his seat to Coe's right. Every man had a flip-top notebook – affectionately called a 'wheel book' – and pen in their hands.

Coe looked around the small space, a copy of their follow-on tasking orders from CINCPACFLT in his hand. Without referring to the paper, his eyes shifted from one face to the next as if trying to assess the mood of each officer. He went to the head of the table. His shoulders appeared bony under the fabric of his shirt and his face looked drawn and gaunt. The ridges of his cheek bones were hard, the sallow flesh stretched thin into stark angles.

"An hour ago, sonar made contact with a large force of enemy surface ships to our south, heading southeast," he said. "CINCPACFLT now believes – and I agree – that what we stumbled on might be part of a Chinese naval assault force massing in the Taiwanese Strait for a probable attack on Taiwan itself," Coe began, then paused to let the information swirl around the room. He saw the Nav and the Engineer exchange dire glances. A couple of men shuffled in their seats and narrowed their eyes.

"We've been ordered to head south towards the Taiwan Strait to engage and sink every enemy vessel we contact. I have no doubt that further south, well beyond the range of our sensors, there are even more enemy ships surging from Chinese ports along the coast and moving eastward. Obviously, we can't sink every ship the enemy puts to sea, but we can put a serious dent in their effort. If this contact does indeed turn out to be a significant number of enemy vessels transiting towards the northern coast of Taiwan, our intervention might make all the difference to the success or failure of the enemy's overall assault plans."

The broad overview completed, Coe paused to allow questions. Only the Weapons Officer spoke. "Sir, has intel confirmed an invasion of Taiwan by the Chinese is imminent?"

"No, I don't believe so," Coe said. "At this stage the first CINCPACFLT knew of the enemy's movements was when we reported the contact. Right now, I imagine every available intelligence asset is hard at work determining the true nature of the force the Chinese are surging, and their intentions. However, their conclusions are irrelevant to this boat. We have our mission, and we have potential targets. The bigger picture is beyond our scope."

Weps nodded. Coe looked for other enquiring faces like he was challenging them, his chin thrust out and the creases at the corners of his mouth picked out in dark shadow. Richard Wickham cleared his throat and asked a question more for the benefit of the rest of the officers than himself. "Do we have a strategy for the attack, sir?"

It was a challenge Chris Coe had been considering privately for the past ten minutes.

"At this stage my plan is to run fast and deep to close the gap on the enemy ships," Coe said simply. "They're angling to the southeast away from us, so it's a high-speed chase. Nav, I want you to work closely with the XO to come up with an intercept course once we get more details on the enemy force composition and approximate speed. If we can't close the gap and lay in wait for them to approach the Taiwanese mainland, we'll launch Harpoons from range and then close to kill the ships we damage. But that's a last resort." Then he turned his eyes onto the Engineer and fixed the man with a steely glare. "Eng, I want you to give me everything from the reactor you've got. Our entire strategy from this moment on will be determined by how quickly we can close the gap on the enemy ships."

"Aye, sir."

"In the meantime," his gaze swept back around the room, addressing everyone, "we pay careful attention to the details, gentlemen. Everything requiring repair or replacement must be seen to. The crew must be rested and fed, and every weapon aboard checked and re-checked. What we do now might save lives when the shooting starts."

*

With *Oklahoma City's* massive powerplant driving the nuc boat through the ocean's depths at more than thirty-three knots, the submarine quickly began making up ground on the enemy flotilla of warships. But there was a trade-off for high speed; *OKC* was announcing her location to any nearby enemy sonar device... and her power plant was generating so much noise that she was all-but acoustically blind to her environment, rendering her sensitive sonar equipment nearly useless except to noisy merchant ships and biologics.

For three tense hours Chris Coe gritted his teeth and allowed *OKC* to dash south, then southeast, fretting incessantly over everything he still did not know about the enemy's composition and location – and fighting a constant battle with himself to show patience and restraint.

Finally, when he could stand the uncertainty no longer, he ordered the boat to reduce speed. "Officer of the Deck, ahead one third."

"Aye, sir."

Coe waited at the conn for several minutes while the ship's speed gradually bled away and then ordered *OKC* to turn east, just long enough for the ship to clear its baffles. "Sonar, conn. Anything behind us?"

"Conn, sonar, negative, sir."

"Very well. OOD, return to course one-eight-seven," Coe said, then reached for the 21MC speaker again. "Sonar, conn. Report all contacts."

"Conn, sonar. We have multiple contacts bearing one-eight-zero, due south. Picking up screw-blade counts for surface vessels. They're doing sixteen knots on multiple five-blade screws with suppressed cavitation."

Coe glanced around the control room and caught the eye of the BSY-1 operators at their consoles. They confirmed the Sonar Sup's call.

"Sonar, aye," Coe said. He strode forward through the sonar shack door and stood behind the sonar operators at their stations. "I need more information," Coe insisted. "Tell me everything you know."

"We're working on it now, sir," the Supervisor kept his voice impassive despite the flush of irritation that burned on his cheeks. Insightful analysis took time. "So far we've classified three contacts as Type 052D *Luyang III*-class destroyers. According to their propeller-blade counts they're making sixteen knots. The other vessel that has been classified is a Type 071 *Yuzhao*-class amphibious transport dock, making fifteen knots. We also have some fixed-wing ASW contacts fading in and out, sir. My guess is that it's shore-based and flying a screen forward of the flotilla."

Coe grunted and went back into control. He strode to the starboard side where the fire control party worked. Four men were at their stations. The screens the men sat in front of were cluttered with data.

Coe glanced sideways at Richard Wickham who was acting FCC. "Well?"

"My best guess, sir, based on the little that we know so far, is that the Chinese have a screen of destroyers ahead of some heavies all heading towards the Taiwan mainland," Richard Wickham said. "The enemy ASW elements overhead might be dropping sonar buoys, though we haven't detected any yet."

"Range to the nearest contact?"

The XO made a call based on the thin stream of data pouring into the submarine's sophisticated computer system and his gut instinct. "If I had to guess, sir, I'd say about sixty-thousand yards. I should be able to firm that range estimate up in another sixty seconds."

Coe made the calculation in his head; thirty-four miles.

"Bearing?"

"Current bearing is one-seven-seven, continuing to draw to the left; to the southeast."

Coe grunted again, then spun on his heel. "Nav, I want a course to put us out in front of the group at twenty-thousand yards so we can get ahead and lay in wait for them to approach us."

Richard Wickham asked a fire control operator to 'trial own ship' to the intercept point on the ship's sophisticated Fire Control system and a moment later imagery appeared on screens in fire control and at the conn. Wickham called across the room to the Nav, "Looks like a course of one-two-zero at twenty-three knots will get us there in forty-four minutes. That will place us twenty-thousand yards ahead of the enemy group."

The Navigation team put the details down on the digital chart to ensure the course was clear of navigation hazards, then confirmed the details to the conn.

"Very good," Coe acknowledged. "Officer of the Deck, make your course one-two-zero, speed thirty knots."

"Aye sir."

Time was now of the essence. Coe still didn't know the exact composition of the enemy flotilla, but he knew more than he did twenty minutes earlier. He now had enough data to confirm sonar's initial call; they had stumbled across a substantial enemy naval force that was steaming for Taiwan.

Now Coe had to maneuver in front of them and lay in wait to spring his trap.

"XO, man battle stations."

*

Oklahoma City reached her station twenty-two thousand yards ahead of the approaching Chinese surface force, and Coe ordered the boat into deep water, watching the secure fathometer readout as the submarine dived lower. At one hundred and eighty feet the water temperature around the submarine began to plunge dramatically, growing progressively colder. Coe saw the sound velocity profile display the readout on a screen just above the helm and made a note of the fact; a strong layer to hide under would make detection from enemy active sonar more difficult.

The submarine settled in deep water with her screws barely turning to maintain headway. The contact with the enemy group was much clearer now with the makeup of the Chinese flotilla becoming more apparent with every passing moment as streams of data poured into sonar and Fire Control.

Behind a screen of three Type 052D *Luyang III*-class destroyers and three more Type 052C *Luyang II*-class destroyers were several major naval vessels including two confirmed Type 071 *Yuzhao*-class amphibious transport docks, a Type 081 Mine Countermeasures vessel, and a massive Type

908 *Fusu*-class Fleet replenishment ship, displacing almost forty-thousand tonnes.

Chris Coe stood at the periscope pedestal and took a long look around the attack center. With the ship at battle stations, every man was waiting in position. The XO, operating as the engagement's fire Control Coordinator, was standing to the starboard side of the conn, forward and directly behind the fire control console operators who were managing or processing new contacts. Weps, as the Weapons Control Coordinator, stood to the right of the conn, aft of the XO. Beside Coe, and standing near the Number Two periscope, the Officer of the Deck waited patiently for the first orders to be given, while around those key men additional junior officers had been assigned to support the Sonar Supervisor, and the fire control operators. Two more junior officers stood at the tactical plotter and there were other junior officers assigned to the torpedo room and to maneuvering.

Twenty-two thousand yards equated to over twelve miles; the approaching enemy group was already well within torpedo range and the distance was closing with every passing minute. Coe turned and addressed the crew.

"Attention in the Attack Center. The approaching Chinese surface group appears to be formed by a line of screening destroyers two miles ahead of a group of heavy support vessels," Coe spoke slowly and deliberately. It was important that he not betray any sense of anxiety. He recognized that this was a moment when the crew needed their CO to be firm and confident; a man in complete control of his emotions. "It is my intention to ignore the enemy destroyers and focus on the heavies. To do that I plan on ascending above the layer again to sharpen our tactical display and to begin zig-zagging the boat across the path of the enemy flotilla in order to confirm target bearings and range." Zig-gagging the submarine across her course track would provide a set of bearing changes to the targets that *OKC's* tracking party could use as a baseline for computing the range to each individual contact. Once that information was confirmed, the submarine could duck back down below the thermal layer to avoid detection until its torpedoes were unleashed. "Are there any questions?"

Coe did not ask for comments. He didn't command by committee.

No one in the Attack Center spoke. The men's faces were tense. Some were sweating while others tried hard to feign indifference. Coe knew better. Every man was keyed up and running on anxiety and adrenaline – himself included.

"Very well. Officer of the Deck, take her up to one-sixty feet."

The boat rose slowly, and the moment it broke through the ocean's thermal layer of cold water, the Sonar Supervisor's voice blared across the 21MC.

"Conn, sonar. I have direct path to the contacts. Bearing to Type 908 *Fusu*-class Fleet replenishment ship, designate Master Thirty is two-eight-four. Bearing to Type 071 *Yuzhao*-class amphibious transport dock, designate Master Thirty-One is two-seven-nine."

"Sonar, aye," Coe acknowledged and moved *Oklahoma City* south a thousand yards before returning to her base course.

"Bearing to second Type 071 *Yuzhao*-class amphibious transport dock, designate Master Thirty-Three is two-six-zero," Sonar added another heavy to the list of enemy ships classified and designated.

Again, Coe moved *OKC* from her base course, traveling two thousand yards northeast.

"Conn, sonar! Several enemy destroyers just lit off their active sonar, sir. They're pinging away with hull and variable depth sonar. Bearings two-eight-one, two-eight-six, and another bearing two-seven-six," the active information displayed on the WLR-9 active intercept receiver.

From Fire Control, Richard Wickham declared, "Sir, we now have ranges confirmed to Master Thirty, Thirty-One and Master Thirty-Two."

"Very well," Coe nodded. He wanted to say more. He wanted to blurt out, *"Thank God!"* and sigh with relief. Instead, he bit the words off and barked at the Chief of the Boat.

"COB, get us back down below the layer. Make your depth four-four-zero feet, all ahead one third. Do it smartly, Mister!"

"Aye, sir!" COB repeated and the orders echoed around the control room in a wave of raised voices.

Coe had everything he needed now to launch his torpedo attacks and expect kills. As the ship plunged back down into the cold depths, he took one last long moment to assess his plan and factor in the risks. The biggest danger to *OKC* would come from the Chinese line of destroyers. Once he launched torpedoes they would swarm like angry wasps, and his entire strategy would depend on his ability to evade detection. He took a careful look at the plot and ruled out any escape to the south; he was sure there were other Chinese warships surging across the Taiwanese Strait. He could not turn east because he would be driven towards shallow water around the coast of Taiwan, and he doubted he could weave a route west through the approaching enemy fleet. That left only north, back into the East China Sea, as a likely escape route.

Oklahoma City was ready to fight, but it was quickly becoming apparent to Chris Coe that not only was the boat hemmed into a tight box, but that soon the walls could very well come crashing in on them...

*

The looming nightmare of being trapped and unable to evade an enemy attack caused Chris Coe to do something he rarely did; he hesitated.

He had originally intended to fire his torpedoes into the Chinese heavies as they approached and then look for an opportunity in the ensuing chaos to steer a course to safety, but now, on the brink of ordering his Mark 48s to shoot, he suddenly reconsidered his options.

His priority was to damage the enemy's possible invasion attempt of Taiwan; that meant sinking or severely damaging the enemy ships that would deliver goods or logistics to the beach or ports for the invasion. The Chinese destroyers were a secondary consideration only.

He was already well within torpedo range. If he fired now, he would most likely get hits, although if the Chinese were alerted to the incoming weapons early, it was still possible the targets could take evasive measures.

If he fired his Harpoons, the launch datum would be instantly seen by the Chinese, both visually and on radar and the Chinese destroyers would swarm forward to maul him. And the Harpoons were no guarantee of target hits, despite their reputation in the media as lethal killers. The fire-and-forget missiles were as likely to strike a destroyer…

Coe discounted a Harpoon attack and re-considered his torpedo options. He could either fire now with good solutions, maintaining the wire to the weapons until the targets were alerted and steal away north, or let the Chinese flotilla drive right over the top of him while he hid deep below the layer. Once the battle group had passed, he could then turn and fire at the Chinese heavies from behind at short range, like a fox that had broken into a henhouse. Allowing the Chinese ships to pass over him and shooting into their baffles would reduce the chance of the enemy ships becoming alerted to the danger of incoming weapons until it was too late for evasion.

The added benefit to the fox in the henhouse scenario – and the one that decided the matter – was the realization that if he fired at the enemy heavies after the flotilla had sailed over him, a second possible escape route opened for him; he could flee west, towards the Chinese mainland before eventually turning back north.

"Attention in the Attack Center," Coe turned and addressed the men. Their faces lifted to him expectantly, each man's expression tight with strain as he began to speak. "We now have good solutions on several key ships in the enemy battle group. However, we're not going to fire," he let that surprising news sink in for a moment and saw expressions of bewilderment on the faces of several junior officers. "Instead, we're going to stay deep and stay quiet, well below the layer, and let the enemy ships drive over the top of us. Once the screen of destroyers and the heavy support ships are to our east and are closing on the Taiwanese mainland, we will rise and turn to fire our weapons at the heavies from behind at close range."

Coe didn't ask for questions or comments. Instead, he turned to the COB. "Chief of the Boat, rig ship for ultra-quiet. Make our depth six-eight-zero."

"Aye, sir," COB said smartly. "Rig ship for ultra-quiet and make my depth six-eight-zero feet."

"Helm ahead one third. Maneuvering make turns for three knots."

"Aye, sir," the orders were repeated.

Oklahoma City glided deeper into the cold depths, the ship slowing gradually until it was barely making headway. Coe studied the navigation plot being displayed around the control room. If the Chinese battle group maintained their current heading, they would pass over *OKC* two thousand yards to the north of her position. He nodded to himself, satisfied.

The tactical decision made, and the orders given, Coe had nothing left to do. He remained standing rigidly at the conn for several seconds until he caught his fingers drumming impatiently on his thigh and he balled his hands into fists.

The torture of waiting through a dull hour for a few seconds of gut-swooping action and fear was the time Coe hated most. There were too many moments where self-doubt and second-guessing could creep into the corners of his mind. To distract himself he calculated the time it would take for the Chinese warships to pass overhead and figured he had another forty minutes until they reached his position, and then perhaps another twenty minutes after that before he could quietly turn behind them and unleash his weapons.

In the sudden empty void of activity Coe felt his tiredness wash over him in waves so strong that he sensed himself physically sway. He was about to order a mess specialist to bring coffee but changed his mind a moment before he gave the command. He needed to be alone. He didn't want the men to see him gripped and trembling with fatigue.

"XO," he announced. "You have the conn. I'll be in the wardroom."

*

Chris Coe got exactly twenty-eight minutes of peace and solitude in the wardroom, nursing a 'blonde and bitter' coffee, before the handset for the JA Command Circuit located beneath the table to the right of the CO's seat buzzed, recalling him to the Control room.

When he entered Control, he noticed the bearing to each Chinese warship was changing steadily from left to right as they approached *Oklahoma City's* position, passed overhead, and then steamed on eastwards towards the Taiwanese mainland.

The noise from the Chinese warships through the submarine was a physical thing; a tremor in the ocean and a rumble of sound that came in relentless waves.

Every man in the Control room held their breath, their eyes lifted to the overhead, tension and a sheen of sweat on their brows. They stood like a group of devoted religious zealots awaiting the wrath of some vengeful god. Their faces flinched and twitched at each new harsh shock of thundering sound lest it be the prelude to a sudden enemy attack.

Coe stood amongst them, his feet leaden and anchored to the deck at the conn, tiny critters of anxiety and apprehension crawling under the skin of his forearms as the tense minutes seemed to stretch for an eternity.

Every vessel in the Chinese battle group had now been classified and allocated a Master number. Coe watched the track of the flotilla on the screen display above the conn, his focus on the three enemy heavies and the Type 081 Mine Countermeasures vessel.

When, finally, the last of the enemy heavies had passed overhead and the noise storm of their passage began to abate,

Coe glanced at his wristwatch. He waited six more minutes. By his calculation the enemy flotilla had traveled another three thousand yards.

"Sonar, conn, bearing to Master Thirty-Two, the Type 908 *Fusu*-class Fleet replenishment ship is zero-nine-two, range twenty-eight hundred yards," the Sonar Sup announced, and then continued listing the bearings and ranges to each of the remaining Chinese heavies.

"Sonar, aye," Coe acknowledged. "Chief of the Boat, make your course zero-nine-zero, depth four-six-zero feet, maintain turns for three knots."

"Aye, sir," COB repeated the orders and they were repeated again, like an echo, as the submarine began to turn and slowly ascend.

"Make tubes one and two ready in all respects, including opening the outer doors."

Richard Wickham passed the order to the torpedo room. "Torpedo room, fire control. Make tubes one and two ready in all respects, including opening the outer doors."

The response was instantaneous. The crew in the torpedo room had been anxiously waiting for the order. "Make tubes one and two ready in all respects, including opening the outer doors. Fire control, Torpedo room, aye."

When the torpedo room acknowledged that the evolution had been completed, the XO passed the report to the conn. "Captain, tubes one and two are ready in all respects. Both outer doors are open. Weapons ready."

"FCC, do you have firing solutions for Master Thirty-One, Master Thirty-Two, Master Thirty-Three and Master Thirty-Four?"

"Aye, sir," Richard Wickham responded.

"Very well," Coe drew a deep breath and squared his shoulders. He wanted to take out the two Type 071 amphibious transport docks with the first salvo. "Fire point procedures, a salvo, Master Thirty-One tube one and Master Thirty-Three tube two. Single Mark 48 ADCAP torpedoes."

"Aye, sir!" the order was repeated.

"Master Thirty-One bearing zero-eight-six, speed fifteen knots, range three thousand yards. Master Thirty-Three bearing zero-nine-five, speed fifteen knots. Range three thousand yards," the XO from Fire Control reported. "Solutions ready!"

"Ship ready!" the Officer of the Deck spoke so quickly that the two men's voices seemed to overlap.

"Weapons ready!" The Weapons Officer said an instant later. The snap in each man's voices reflected the tension that had built over the past arduous hour of fretful apprehension. Everyone in Control was wound tight as a spring.

Coe nodded. He felt a nerve at the corner of his eye tick involuntarily. "Sonar, conn, stand by."

"Conn, sonar, standing by."

"Match sonar bearings and shoot tube one, Master Thirty-One, the Type 071!"

"Set!" The Fire Control Coordinator said.

Up until this moment the system solution had been generated on a bearing to the contact that had been based on the estimated TMA solution, which was often slightly different than the target data. A Fire Control operator entered the most recent sonar bearings into the system.

"Standby," Weps ordered.

The operator moved the firing switch to the 'standby' position until he saw a sudden flashing light on his panel indicating 'Interlocks closed'.

"Interlocks closed," the operator made the call, verifying that all doors were open, and the launch system was ready.

"Shoot!"

The operator sitting in front of where Weps stood pressed the 'firing' key, and the Control room filled with the swelling sounds of rumbling air noses. Chris Coe's ears popped.

The submarine shuddered as the first Mk 48 burst from its torpedo tube. The Combat Systems Officer confirmed the launch. "Tube one fired electrically. Impulse return, normal launch, good wire."

"Torpedo course zero-eight-six, speed twenty-five knots and accelerating. Descending to search depth."

"Match sonar bearings and shoot tube two, Master Thirty-Three, the Type 071!"

"Set!" FCC said, and the carefully orchestrated firing procedure was repeated a second time.

"Shoot!" Weps said.

Again, the huge submarine shuddered from stem to stern as the ADCAP Mk 48 torpedo was thrust violently from its launch tube.

"Tube two fired electrically," the CSO confirmed the second successful launch. "Impulse return, normal launch, good wire."

"Torpedo course zero-nine-five, speed twenty-three knots and accelerating. Weapon is descending to search depth," a combat system operator said.

Both of the Mk 48s completed their wire-clearance maneuvers and ran at high speed for their separate targets.

"Time to enable?" Coe needed to know. It wouldn't be long – not at such close range.

"Forty seconds, Captain."

"Very well."

"Conn, sonar," it was the Sonar Supervisor's voice on the 21MC. "Hold both weapons running at high speed and now enabling."

The control room remained quiet as an open grave until a Combat System Operator announced in a voice brimming with savage satisfaction, "First weapon, detect! detect! Homing, bearing zero-eight-six, speed fifteen knots, range three thousand yards. Weapon is going shallow."

"Matches solution for Master Thirty-One," Richard Wickham said. "No steer required."

"Conn, sonar. The first weapon has acquired Master Thirty-One, the Type 071. Torpedo increasing speed."

"Sonar, aye. Any indication of alertment?"

"No, sir. Target is still bearing zero-eight-six."

Coe grunted. In his mind's eye he could see the torpedo, hunting through the water like a shark on the scent of blood, racing towards the blunt stern of the enemy warship. He visualized the vessel's foaming wide wake and the torpedo following that unmistakable trail, relentless and lethal.

"Conn, sonar. The second weapon has acquired Master Thirty-Three, the Type 071, bearing zero-nine-five."

"Fire control, time to impact both torpedoes?" Coe wanted confirmation of the predictive data he could see on the display screens surrounding the conn.

"One minute fifty seconds, sir," Richard Wickham confirmed.

"Very well. Make tubes three and four ready in all respects."

The orders were repeated, acknowledged, and the evolution attended to quickly by the men working themselves to a frenzy in the torpedo room. Coe waited impatiently.

"Captain, tubes three and four are ready. Both outer doors are open. The room is ready."

"Fire point procedures, Master Thirty-Two tube three and Master Thirty-Four tube four. Single Mark 48 ADCAP torpedoes."

"Aye, sir!"

"Master Thirty-Two bearing zero-nine-two, course zero nine-zero, speed fifteen, range three-five-hundred yards. Master Thirty-Four bearing zero-nine-nine, course zero-nine-zero, speed fifteen. Range four thousand yards," the XO reported. "Solutions ready!"

"Ship ready!"

"Weapons ready!"

"Sonar, conn, stand by," Coe was caught up in the blood-lust of combat.

"Conn, sonar, standing by."

"Match sonar bearings and shoot tube three, Master Thirty-Two, the Type 908 *Fusu*-class!"

"Set!"

"Shoot!" Weps growled at the conclusion of the firing procedure.

The Mk 48 was unleashed from its torpedo tube. The Combat Systems Officer confirmed the launch.

"Match sonar bearings and shoot tube four, Master Thirty-Four, the Type 081!"

"Set!" Richard Wickham confirmed.

"Interlocks closed," the operator confirmed that the launch system was ready.

"Shoot!" Weps ordered the fourth Mk 48 fired.

"Tube two fired electrically. Impulse return, normal launch, good wire," the tone of triumph in the young Combat Systems Officer was unmistakable.

"Conn, sonar. Hold both weapons running at high speed and now enabling."

A moment later the CSO reported torpedoes three and four had both detected their targets and were homing.

"Weps! Cut the wires. Shut all outer doors. Reload all torpedo tubes!" Coe snapped.

Everything seemed to be happening at once and it took cool, well-trained men to work effectively in the chaos of a Control Room in a combat situation. There was a buzz of frantic activity; a wall of purposefully intense noise. Yet through the apparent upheaval everything necessary was being accomplished with professionalism. It was a measure of the crew's relentless training and a mark of the US submarine force's superiority over other world forces. Now the relentless drills and the endless hours of rehearsal and repetition were paying dividends in precious time.

"Chief of the Boat, make your course two-seven-zero, increase speed to flank."

"Aye, sir." More voices added to the clamor as the orders were echoed.

No sooner had the submarine begun to increase speed and begin turning her bow towards the west than the voice of the Sonar Supervisor seemed to overwhelm everything else.

"Conn, sonar! Multiple surface explosions bearing zero-eight-eight and zero-nine-five. The first two weapons have struck their targets. Master Thirty-One making break-up sounds. I think she's a goner. Master Thirty-Three struck by several secondary... holy shit! She's just blown wide open, sir!"

"FCC! Time to impact Masters Thirty-Two and Thirty-Four?"

"Fifty-five seconds, sir!" Richard Wickham was perhaps the most overworked man in the Control room at that moment, yet he kept his voice calm and unflustered, making the difficult work appear deceptively easy.

Coe hesitated.

The Chinese skippers aboard the Type 81 Mine Countermeasures vessel and the massive Type 908 *Fusu*-class Fleet replenishment ship would both now be alerted to the imminent danger and trying to take desperate evasive measures.

Was there anything the Chinese could do in less than fifty seconds to save their ships from almost certain destruction?

Coe doubted it, but he was torn between ensuring his weapons struck their targets and the very urgent need to clear datum. The Chinese destroyers would have heard the explosions and by now at least four of them would be turning hard astern and beginning to hunt for him. In another five minutes the ocean around *Oklahoma City* would be thick with enemy warships and the sky overhead buzzing with helicopters.

He made his decision. This wasn't a suicide mission.

"Launch countermeasures," Coe said suddenly. The noisemakers might buy him the few extra precious seconds he needed to make good his evasion.

The order was repeated crisply by the COB. The launcher was located where Weps was stationed. He fired two ADC Mk3 tubes from their dispensers. The ADCs activated immediately.

"Conn, sonar. Explosion on the surface, bearing zero-nine-two. It's the Type 908 *Fusu*-class, sir. She's just taken a direct hit. Weapon three has impacted. Two large explosions but the sound is turning confused in our baffles." The submarine's acoustic ability was being smothered by the sound of the submarine accelerating, the noise of secondary explosions from the already sinking Type 71 amphibious transport docks and the approaching bellow through the water of the Chinese destroyers, charging to the hunt.

"Sonar, aye," Coe responded. *Oklahoma City* had done all she could do. The attack was over. Now they must desperately fight for survival.

Chapter 10:

The Chinese destroyers responded with shock and then outrage to the sudden series of torpedo explosions that ripped through the flotilla. Two of the Type 052C *Luyang II*-class destroyers turned and surged into the smoking, flaming nightmare of debris, searching for survivors of the explosions. The huge Type 908 *Fusu*-class Fleet replenishment ship had been struck astern, tearing a huge hole in the ship's hull below the waterline, destroying her engines and igniting fuel and cargo. She was sinking slowly, her hull streaked and blackened, her stern down in the water and her bow thrusting towards the sky as she began to sink. The ocean around the vast ship was a white foaming maelstrom of debris, burning wreckage and scorched dead bodies.

One of the Type 071 amphibious transport docks had already sunk with only a drifting black scar of oily smoke to mark her watery grave. The second Type 071 was listing heavily to port, her stern aflame and her superstructure hidden behind three towering columns of oily haze. The ship's hull was streaked with cascades of white fire-suppressing foam. Terrified crewmen were lined up along the ship's railing, clambering to throw themselves into the churning ocean before the vessel sank. Wailing alarm sirens sounded, adding their strident noise to the cataclysmic confusion. One of the Chinese destroyers pulled alongside the stricken warship but was pushed back by the intensity of the flames. The water was a junkyard of twisted wreckage and covered in a film of oil. Thick smoke and choking fumes ebbed and swirled as the destroyer's skipper conned his vessel into the chaos.

The remaining four Chinese destroyers, including the three sophisticated Type 052D *Luyang III*-class warships raced west in pursuit of *Oklahoma City*. The Type 052D was a larger variant of the 052C and used a cannister-type vertical launching system. The ships were fitted with flat-paneled active electronically scanned array radar and had been touted by the Chinese as the 'Chinese Aegis' – comparing it to America's *Arleigh Burke*-class destroyers.

The destroyers were armed with CY-5 solid fueled anti-submarine missiles and integrated two Type 7424B triple torpedo tubes for launching Yu-7 torpedoes.

Six minutes after the first ship in the flotilla had exploded a Chinese destroyer launched its Ka-28 'Helix' helicopter from the ship's stern flight deck. The helo was armed with a Russian-designed APR-3E airborne light ASW acoustic homing torpedo, designed to engage enemy submarines at depths up to eight hundred meters at speeds above fifty knots. The helo flew directly west. Two minutes later the remaining Type 052D destroyers launched their own helicopters and the deadly hunt for *OKC* began in earnest.

Five hundred and forty feet below the churning surface of the ocean, *Oklahoma City* was on course two-seven-zero, heading due west at flank speed. Coe was aware the eerie tranquility could not last, and he was wary of travelling in straight lines for too long. He also knew that flank speed had a downside; *Oklahoma City* was more detectable acoustically to the enemy from its fast-speed pumps.

Now the submarine had cleared datum and was eight thousand yards west of the submarine's firing point he checked his wristwatch. Seven fraught, anxious minutes had passed since his weapons launch. In his mind a battle-clock was ticking; calculating the Chinese response time, the delay before the enemy launched its helos, and guestimating their probable search pattern. It was like staring down a bullet; trying to sense the instant before the other guy pulled the trigger. If he reacted too soon, he might stumble into a trap. If he reacted too late, he would take a fatal hit.

He counted down the seconds, each passing moment seeming to increase the tension. The longer he delayed, the more silent alarms sounded in his subconscious.

"Chief of the Boat, make your course two-nine-five! All ahead one third. Have maneuvering shift pumps to slow."

"Aye, sir!" COB's voice betrayed his relief. Every man in control was acutely aware of the life-and-death game being played out. COB repeated the orders and the helmsman reacted quickly.

Oklahoma City turned onto her new course, angling more towards the north and slowing speed dramatically to increase her stealth. *OKC* could never win a race to safety. She had cleared datum – now Chris Coe must use cunning and patience to break free of the encircling arms of the enemy.

The SSN's greatest advantage in warfare, and in the need of evasion, was her silence – but stealth came at the cost of speed. The submarine slowed and the ambient sound of her powerplant through the Control room subsided until Coe was sure he could hear the thump of his heart pounding inside the cage of his chest.

As soon as the submarine began slowing, sonar started picking up the faint sounds of approaching Chinese helicopters.

"Conn, sonar. Helo bearing one-one-zero and closing. He's flying low. Another helo contact bearing one-eight-five, but I think he's moving away, further to the south."

"Sonar, aye," Coe acknowledged.

"Conn, sonar. Fly over from forward to aft."

"Sonar, aye," Coe acknowledged again. Streaking lines showed on the sonar display in Control.

A moment later the Sonar Supervisor's voice was tense with alarm. "Conn, sonar. Multiple sonobuoys being dropped to the south!" The bearings for the sonobuoys were simultaneously 'buzzed' to the FCC so the locations appeared in the ship's fire control system.

"Right full rudder!" Coe reacted.

One of the sonobuoys deployed five hundred yards from the submarine and the jarring metallic tone of its pings was like the sound of scratched fingernails down a blackboard in the Control room.

"Conn, sonar. Surface splashes…"

The chances were good that the sonobuoy dropped from the Ka-28 had found the *Oklahoma City*, but Coe held his nerve until the Sonar Supervisor's voice shattered the brittle silence.

"Conn, sonar. Splash and engine start-up! Torpedo in the water. Torpedo bearing one-two-zero!"

The enemy helo had launched its APR-3E acoustic torpedo. Coe visualized the tactical display in his mind's eye. *OKC* had turned hard right and was now steering zero-one-five, almost due north. The Chinese torpedo was approaching it broadside from the southeast. "Come to new course two-eight-zero. All ahead flank!" Coe had no choice. *OKC* was completely on the defensive. He turned the boat to the northwest to put the torpedo on the edge of the submarine's port baffles.

For a submarine commander almost every tactical consideration revolved around a compass rose and a line of sight. *Instinct* told Coe that the optimum course was the reciprocal bearing to the torpedo, allowing him to move at best speed directly away from the threat. But to do so would compromise the 'line of sight' to the torpedo and put the danger directly into his baffles where he would be blind to its movement. *Intuition* told Coe the solution was to turn away and position the torpedo to a point less directly astern from where sonar could still track its approach.

The APR-3E acoustic homing torpedo launched from the Chinese helo splashed down into the ocean, the control surfaces of the weapon enabling the torpedo to travel in a spiral path without starting the engine. The acoustic seeker in the weapon began searching for targets and once it identified *OKC*, the engines started, and the solid propellant rocket engine kicked the weapon into a high-speed attack.

"High-frequency pinging," the Sonar Sup warned. "The enemy torpedo has acquired us."

The news was confirmed by the WLR-9 display that showed the enemy torpedoe's increasing SNR on the Sound Pressure Level, and the changing of the ping intervals as they became progressively shorter. Then the pulse length and type altered, shifting from a CW to an FM pulse which could be heard through *OKC's* hull.

Sonar identified the enemy torpedo by its signature sound and Coe racked his brain for everything he could recall about the weapon. He knew it had a top speed of over fifty knots and that the seeker range was somewhere between one and two kilometers. *But the torpedo's operational range?* He drew a momentary mental blank and a white-cold fist of panic gripped him. For three thumping heartbeats he stood frozen until at last he recalled the torpedo's critical data: *thirty-five hundred yards.*

"Torpedo is closing! Range three thousand yards!"

Coe's eyes flashed to the old analogue compass rose in the overhead display, located forward of the Number Two Scope to make certain he knew his course and the bearing drift of the torpedo. Nearby digital displays showed the enemy torpedo as it hunted towards the submarine. Coe did the arithmetic in his head and checked it twice. If he maintained flank speed, the enemy weapon would run out of fuel before it caught the submarine. He had just drawn a relieved breath when the voice of the Sonar Supervisor sounded a fresh alert.

"Conn, sonar! A second torpedo in the water! Torpedo bearing one-eight-two. Range two-thousand yards. It's another helo-launched APR-3E, sir! It went active a few moments after it hit the ocean."

Christ!

"Sonar, aye," Coe acknowledged and drew his lips into a thin pale line of tension. He had to wait; he had to hold his course until the first torpedo had run out of fuel and sunk harmlessly to the ocean floor. He spun around and stared at the sonar monitor on the conn. A bright white spoke of light was glowing on the display, denoting the second torpedo. Coe made another quick calculation. The second torpedo was closing at a rate of about a thousand yards every minute. In two minutes *OKC* would be destroyed.

"Launch countermeasures!" despite himself Coe could not contain the edge of anxiety in his voice. The two ADC Mk3 deployed astern of the submarine and began emitting a frenzy of acoustic noise.

"Conn, sonar. Torpedo one is slowing and losing contact, sir. I think she's run out of steam. Torpedo two approaching the countermeasures."

Coe held his breath. The Chinese torpedo burst through the two American noisemakers and came surging on, still homing relentlessly on USS *Oklahoma City*.

"Rig ship for high speed!"

"Aye, sir!"

Quickly a series of mechanical stops inside the ship were automatically placed at the hydraulic rams controlling the rudder and stern planes. The stops served to minimize the submarine's maneuverability at high speed to reduce the risk of the stern planes failing and sending the submarine into an unrecoverable dive.

"Fish tail the rudder!"

"Aye, sir!"

The 688 *Los Angeles*-class submarines had a huge rudder and moving the rudder several degrees from port to starboard created a massive wall of disturbed water behind the ship without dramatically compromising her speed.

The submarine slewed in the ocean as she swung from port to starboard. The Chinese torpedo ploughed through the disturbance undeterred.

"Secure ship from high speed!"

"Aye, sir!"

"Fire second salvo of noise makers!" Coe snapped the order. "COB, hard right rudder! Rig ship for impact!"

The submarine turned violently in the ocean, heeling over at a thirty-degree angle and leaving a deep effervescing knuckle in its wake.

"Steer zero-nine-zero!" Coe put the submarine on an easterly course, turning back towards the sinking enemy ships that *OKC* had torpedoed. Coe paused for an instant, undecided about the submarine's depth. It was his belief – with some real-world experience – that many foreign torpedoes were not well maintained. American torpedoes routinely were put through a stringent quality assurance process, including testing them in water before returning them to inventory. If the second salvo of noisemakers did not distract the incoming torpedo, his last 'Hail Mary' chance for evasion was to go as deep as he could in the hope the enemy weapon would leak and fail under massive undersea pressures.

Coe drew a breath, about to give the order to take the boat into a steep dive.

The Chinese APR-3E reached the second pair of ADC Mk3 countermeasures and the huge growling knuckle of noise and bubbles the submarine had left astern – *and detonated.*

The shock wave of the near-miss explosion hammered the hull of the *Oklahoma City;* a brutal battering of thundering noise and a violent upheaval that seemed to push the massive submarine sideways in the ocean. The effect was quake-like. Every man in the conn was thrown to the deck. Someone cried out in sudden agony and bright red blood spilled. An operator in fire control slammed his head against the desk of his workstation and reeled away clutching at his face with blood streaming between his fingers. Lights blew, others flickered, and electrical sparks hissed and fizzed. Chris Coe was thrown bodily across the Control room. He felt his shoulder slam into a hydraulic valve and a wicked jolt of electric pain lanced up his arm and exploded in pinwheels of light behind his eyes. He scrambled to his knees, his vision swimming. The deck beneath him seemed canted. He pushed himself to his feet and swayed. The Control room looked like the aftermath of a grenade explosion. Men were strewn across the deck in attitudes of agony. In the background emergency alarms were sounding through the length of the ship. Coe took four staggering steps to the conn.

"Chief of the Watch, all stations report damage!" Coe's injured arm hung limp against his side and when he looked, he saw a gash through the torn fabric of his sleeve that was dripping blood. Around him men were dragging themselves to their feet. COB had a hand to his forehead, his face pallid, as if he had been bled from the jugular.

One of the watch standers in shaft alley picked up the 4MC emergency reporting circuit and his voice carried to every part of the ship. "Emergency report! Emergency report. *Flooding* in the engine room," his voice was ragged and thick with panic. "Flooding from the shaft seals!"

Shaft alley was the most remote place in the engine room. Here, at the very stern of the boat, all three engineering deck levels came together to support the shaft exiting the ship. The upper level that housed the turbines had stairs that descended to the middle level and the stairwell continued to the lower level where the ship's oil systems were housed. All this machinery was crammed together in a shaft of space about fifty feet long. On the starboard side stood an array of large ship's service hydraulic pumps, and on the port side were the large steering and diving pumps that generated high hydraulic pressure for the rudder and planes. Between these two massive banks of pumps was the ship's monstrous shaft; measuring almost three feet in diameter, running from the prop to the main thrust bearing almost a hundred feet into the engine room spaces.

A moment later maneuvering paralleled the watch stander's report and a moment after that the Chief of the Watch sounded the 'collision-flooding alarm'. A dreaded wailing tone sounded through the ship.

"Flooding in the engine room," the COW announced.

Flooding from the shaft seals!

In the submarine force, the word 'flooding' was dramatic. It was only ever used if the damage to the vessel was catastrophic and lives were in imminent danger. Once heard in Control, the term 'flooding in the engine room' automatically triggered an emergency blow to get the submarine to the surface immediately.

Chris Coe overrode the command. His eyes locked on to the Chief of the Watch who was standing with his hands on the blow valves – called the 'chicken switches' by the enlisted crew. The riveting force of Coe's glare froze the man. *"COW do not emergency blow!"*

Coe's eyes hunted around the conn until he found Richard Wickham. The XO was on his knees between the plot tables; his face wrenched tight in a rictus of pain. He came to his feet slowly and took a couple of drunken steps.

"XO, there is flooding in the engine room. I am overriding the command for an emergency blow," Coe said stiffly. "You have the deck and the conn. Get the ship up to one-fifty feet and work with maneuvering once they recover the engine room to get out of here at best speed. I need you to keep us afloat and alive while I go aft to assess the situation."

"Sir, I can –"

"No!" Coe barked. He wouldn't trust anyone else to oversee the repair attempts; not with the survival of the boat on the line. *I have to do this.*

*

The first designs for the SSN-688 *Los Angeles*-class of fast attack submarines came off the shipwrights drawing boards back in the early 1970s when the Navy was desperately in need of a fast submarine that could keep pace with a growing fleet of nuclear-powered aircraft carriers. As such, the design featured a myriad of compromises. The essence was a relatively light-weight submarine that carried a massive nuclear reactor. The trade-off to increase speed was weight reduction, and one of the ways the designers were able to minimize the submarine's weight was by eliminating a number of water-tight bulkheads through the length of the boat.

Compared to a typical WW2 diesel boat that had around seven water-tight compartments, weighed around seventeen-hundred tons and had a speed of about eight knots submerged, the SSN-688 nucs were Ferraris.

The finished *Los Angeles*-class submarines were launched with only two water-tight compartments. The one water-tight door on the boat separated the engineering from the operations compartment and was situated aft of the crew's mess, on the starboard side of the boat. The water-tight door opened into a narrow passageway which passed along the outside of the submarine's normally-locked reactor compartment. When Coe arrived at the bulkhead. the door was manned by a young Ensign and dogged shut by procedure.

The young sailor's face was white with rising panic. All around the submarine alarms were sounding and warning lights flashing. Through the bullseye window set into the heavy steel door he could see men in the engine spaces rushing to get damage control equipment and then dash aft. The Ensign's eyes were huge and hectic. He saw Chris Coe approaching with a forward damage control party around him, and his face began working in agitation.

"Open the water-tight door," Coe demanded. "And once we're in engineering, close it behind us again. Understand, sailor?"

"Aye, sir," the Ensign blurted. He undogged the door slightly and a huge rush of foul-smelling air pressure from the ocean coming into the engine room washed over them like a howling gale.

Coe gritted his teeth and waded into the maelstrom.

"Shut the door!" he turned back and had to shout to be heard.

The young Ensign threw his weight behind the door. Coe watched the tiny sliver of light shrink and felt a sudden claustrophobic sensation of rising panic. The door finally closed with a muffled *'clang!'* and the sensation of being sealed in a tomb overwhelmed him.

In the flickering overhead light of the engine room, he could see crewmen working with frantic panic to reach the control panels to operate the pumps while other crewmen were moving about the engineering spaces to reopen large steam valves to bring steam back into the giant turbines for propulsion and electricity. In the midst of the chaotic activity stood the Engineering Watch Supervisor, a tall thin man in his thirties, wringing wet, his knuckles bloodied and grazed, and his face smeared with grease. As Coe strode deeper into the desperate clamor, he heard the EWS swearing. The man saw Coe out of the corner of his eye and straightened. His face took on the expression of a surgeon about to deliver an anxious patient the very worst possible news.

"It's bad, sir," the EWS had no time for pleasantries or procedure. He was a Machinist's Mate Master Chief and the senior enlisted member of a nine-man watch team. "I've just come back from shaft alley and made a report to the EOOW in maneuvering. Water is pouring through the forward shaft seals. I've got guys trying to tighten them and we're pumping the bilge with the drain pump. The next step will be to inflate the boot and see if we can stem the flooding. We've already tried that once but it didn't work…"

"How did it happen?"

"My guess is that the violent shock cracked the seal faces. When that happened there was nothing left in place around the shaft to prevent seawater pouring in."

The submarine's shaft seals were wrapped around the vessel's propeller shaft in a series of carbon bands. They were made to barely touch the shaft as it rotated without creating excessive noise. The bands were spaced apart, and on each side, seawater was introduced via a network of piping in a way that used the ocean's own pressure to keep the seawater out. Successively, between each band, the amount of seawater allowed to leak was decreased until the final seal inside the submarine's hull is almost water-tight.

The EWS led Coe towards shaft alley and – despite himself and the dire horror of the emergency situation – Coe was, as always, awe-struck by the size and complexity of the submarine's engine room. From the water-tight door to the stern of the ship was almost two hundred feet of multi-leveled engine space filled with massive machinery, pumps, plant equipment and a myriad of piping and valves. It was like standing in the entrance of a vast cathedral, filled with steel.

"We're getting every pump working at capacity, but we're losing the fight to keep the water from filling the engine room lower level and grounding out all the hydraulic pumps."

Coe looked around in rising despair. Every minute the ship continued to flood the weight of a large dump truck filled with sand was being shipped aboard the submarine. He imagined Richard Wickham in the Control room and the Diving Officer of the Watch beside him, fretfully studying the ship's trim angle as more and more water surged aboard and *OKC* inevitably began to sink by the stern.

The engine space around the submarine's propeller shaft was surrounded by a damage-control party wielding tools, while water surged like from a broken fire hydrant. Several of the men shouldered large green bags filled with wooden plugs, wire, duct tape and hammers – anything that might be useful. As Coe watched, one of the crewmen reeled away, clutching at his arm, his scream of agony drowned out by the roar of the gushing water. The crewman staggered and then fell below the surface of the water. Another man threw down his tools and heaved the fallen man out of the thick stinking scum of oil and diesel.

The Engineering Watch Supervisor directed the damage control party that Coe had brought with him to join the team of crewmen working around the shaft. Chris Coe waded after them. Something snagged his leg and the bitter cold stung like a razor slash, but there was no more pain. He slapped the EWS hard on the shoulder to get his attention. The water was rising around them at an alarming rate. Now they were waist-deep in the frigid brine and Coe's lower body was so numb with the cold that he could no longer feel his legs. Coe was appalled at how quickly the water level in shaft alley was climbing.

"Get everyone out who isn't necessary. Evacuate them now. I want just enough machinists' mates left behind to make another attempt to inflate the emergency bladder."

The EWS started pushing men away from the shaft and ordering them out of engineering, shouting himself hoarse against the roaring torrent of noise and water to be heard. Equipment began grounding and then two small electrical fires flared in the gloom behind thin feathers of grey smoke. Chris

Coe waded to a handset, grunting with the physical effort necessary, and tried to contact the Control room. For a moment the line buzzed and crackled in his ear then cut out completely. Coe cursed. He threw down the handset and seized the Damage Control phone talker who was wearing a voice-powered headset. He gripped the man by the forearm and pulled the crewman's face close to his. "Is Control on the line?"

"No, sir. I'm still trying…"

"Forget it! The phones are grounded out, so I want you to go forward and get a message to Control. The water-tight bulkhead door is to be shut and dogged behind you – and it doesn't get opened again until the ship has reached safety. Understand?"

The crewman was soaked to the bone, his jaw clenched tight with pain and his face bleeding from several cuts. But he understood the enormity of what the Captain was ordering. His features contorted.

The crewman went silent for an incredulous second and then covered his shock with a despairing protest. "But, sir!"

"I mean it," Coe growled.

The trail of weary, exhausted men reached the bulkhead and the massive door swung open.

"Control, this is Ensign Latham at the water-tight door stationed by the aft bulkhead," the man rasped through great lungsful of gulping air. "Message from the Captain, sir. He has ordered the water-tight bulkhead door to remain sealed and dogged down until the ship can reach safety."

Richard Wickham answered the call. He snatched up the sound phone and spoke quickly. "How bad is the damage?"

"It's pretty bad," the Ensign understated. "Water is now waist deep in shaft alley and the PLO bay… and still rising. The forward shaft seal is gone. We've got two or three cracked shaft seals. The trim pump and the drain pump are both working at maximum capacity and there are electric portable pumps connected with hoses and lined up to pump the bilges, but they're still not keeping up with the amount of water being shipped aboard."

"Where is the Captain?"

"He's still in the engine room engineering spaces, sir. He's working with a damage control party and the EWS. They're making a last desperate attempt to inflate the shaft boot to stop the flooding."

"And the Captain ordered the water-tight bulkhead door dogged down and not to be opened again?" Richard Wickham understood immediately what that meant. Coe had just signed death warrants for every man still in engineering, including himself.

"Yes, sir."

"Belay that order, Mister!" Richard Wickham barked. "I want another damage control party and two divers at that water-tight door in three minutes. Comms are going down across the ship, so it's up to you, Ensign Latham. Find the men and have them waiting at that bulkhead door for my orders!"

Chapter 11:

There was eight of them; six machinist's mates, the Engineering Watch supervisor, and Chris Coe. Together, and with every muscle straining against the weight of the inflatable boot and the sucking draw of the rising water around their chests, they worked desperately to get the massive rubber bladder prepared for inflation. The area around the shaft was a nightmare of plant equipment and shelves of stored spare parts, making it cramped and claustrophobic – like working in a narrow gorge surrounded by cliffs of heavy steel and boxes of machinery.

It took four frantic lung-burning minutes of effort before the boot was properly positioned between the hull where the shaft penetrated the ship and the after-shaft seal. Coe reeled away, his chest heaving like a bellows. His knuckles were grazed and there was a tinge of red blood in the oily surface scum of the wallowing water that lapped around him. The EWS's face was streaked with grime, the man's features drawn and etched with deeply-cut lines of exhaustion.

"We've got to get to the inflating valves!" the EWS shouted over the surging roar of the incoming water.

"Where are they?" Coe shouted back.

The EWS looked pained. He pointed. "They're under water. They're all the way aft against the bulkhead and low in the shaft alley bilge."

"Christ!"

Two machinist's mates were old hands, and they knew the ship's engineering spaces intimately. Standing side-by-side, the water rising to their shoulders, they filled their lungs with air and then ducked below the surface. The water was black with oil and thick with particles of floating debris. They had to work by touch alone, feeling their way between and then through a complex network of piping as they groped to find the air valves with their free hands.

Suddenly one of the men burst through the surface, gasping and retching. His hair was matted black in a thick slime of oil that streaked in rivulets down his face. His lips were purple, his face blanched white by the biting cold.

"Is it done?" Coe barked.

The machinist's mate didn't answer. He snatched three quick breaths and plunged back down into the heaving brine.

Coe counted down the seconds, each one a fresh agony of biting cold and rising alarm. Finally, the two men surfaced twenty feet away, on the far side of the massive shaft. They were exhausted, their lungs on fire. One of the men clung to a heavy pipe and retched violently.

"It's done!" the second man rasped. He had a cut over his right eye and his brow was streaming bright red blood. He seemed to sway on his feet and then his legs gave way. He slipped below the surface for a moment and then came up again, coughing and choking.

There was a fresh sound now; a noise other than the hissing fury of the ruptured seals. It was the sound of compressed air flooding into the massive rubber boot. Coe reached around under the filthy water until he felt the edge of the bladder. He held his hand in place. The rubber skin seemed alive as the air filled it and it began to take firm shape. Quickly the EWS and the nearest machinist's mates waded forward to tighten the circular band around the shaft against the inrushing water.

"Okay!" he gave the EWS the thumbs-up. He scraped oily grime from his face with the back of his hand and pointed forward. "Let's get everyone to safety. There's nothing we can do now except hope it –"

The stern of the submarine suddenly shivered as if it had been picked up by some mythical underwater monster and shaken. For three terrifying seconds the hull shimmied inexplicably from side to side. One of the shelves overhanging the crowded space swayed and a stack of heavy bearing parts fell, splashing into the water. The boxes rained down like incoming artillery. One of them struck Chris Coe on the head, splitting his skull open. He cried out in agony as the world around him turned red with blood and then pitch black…

*

"There are eight men trapped in engineering," Richard Wickham stood by the water-tight bulkhead door and addressed the forward damage control team and the two divers. "One of them is the Captain. I want them all out – immediately. They're working in shaft alley. Go in and get them!"

The heavy door was undogged and the damage control party raced aft into danger. Richard Wickham stood by the door. He could hear a clamor of noise coming from further aft and the unmistakable sound of rushing water. Then the deck beneath him shivered and he had to reach for a handhold to keep his balance.

"What the fuck..?" the words were torn from his lips. He reached frantically for the handset by the door and called the conn. Weps answered from control.

"What happened?" Wickham demanded.

"Don't know," Weps said. He sounded panicked and disorientated. "We're going down. Depth is two-twenty feet and increasing. It might have –" the sound-powered phone connection gave out suddenly.

Wickham hesitated, torn between his duty to the ship and to the men he had just sent into the jaws of danger. He stood his ground.

The first of the machinist's mates appeared out of the gloom, staggering forward towards the water-tight door two minutes later. They were broken with exhaustion, their legs rubbery beneath them, soaking wet and streaked with oily grime. Three of the men were bleeding, and another nursed a broken arm. Their faces were wrenched tight in agony. They lurched through the open door and collapsed in the passageway. Richard Wickham sent Ensign Latham to fetch the ship's doctor.

"Where is the Captain?" the XO seized the nearest man and shook him. "Where is Captain Coe?"

"He's still in there," the machinist's mate pointed. His thickly-muscled arm was covered in faded tattoos. "He got hit on the head by a falling box of bearings. He was knocked unconscious."

The rest of the men emerged from the gloom of the engine space in twos and threes, damage control party members carrying the survivors forward, some limping, some sobbing with exhaustion. The two divers brought Chris Coe out, carrying him between them. The Captain's face was awash with a bloody mask, his lower left leg also bleeding. He lay unmoving as the divers heaved him through the water-tight door.

"Get him to the wardroom!" Wickham barked. In emergencies the table in the wardroom doubled as an operating table. "And get the Doc to him immediately."

The EWS was the last man through the water-tight door. He slumped against the narrow passageway bulkhead and bent forward at the waist to retch. "The boot is in place and it's inflating," he said between gulping painful breaths.

*

Richard Wickham ordered the water-tight door re-dogged and then turned on his heel and raced towards Control. When he entered the room, the scene was a chaos of alarms and faltering electrical circuits. The Diving Officer of the Watch and the COW stood, their eyes glued to the display that showed the ship's depth.

Oklahoma City was sinking by the stern, dropping through three-hundred feet.

"Passing three-five-zero feet and still descending," the COB intoned morosely, his voice like a slow-tolling bell of doom.

Richard Wickham snatched a handset for the JA command circuit from its bracket.

"Maneuvering, conn. This is the XO."

"Conn, maneuvering, aye."

Throughout the flooding crisis at the stern of the ship the Engineering Officer of the Watch and three watch standers had remained in the maneuvering room to monitor the status of the nuclear reactor and coordinate with the OOD, during Wickham's brief absence, on how to save the ship. The EOOWs focus was on attempting to recover the engine room as quickly as possible. The first step in the process was to get the steam system back up and operating so that the ship could make electricity, and then to get the propulsion turbines back online.

"Maneuvering I need propulsion. We're going down and I can't do anything to save the boat until you get those engines back on line," Wickham's voice was tight with strain.

There was an alternative, and for a long moment Wickham considered ordering maneuvering to rig out the outboard and shifting to remote.

The submarine's 'outboard' or SPM (secondary propulsion motor) could be lowered out of the ballast tanks near the stern. It was a 325hp electric AC motor and trainable to any direction by remote control. The outboard was normally used for maneuvering the submarine around the pier when entering or leaving port... but to deploy the unit required it to be lowered and tested in shaft alley – right where men were risking their lives to repair the cracked shaft sealed.

The XO discounted the notion. He didn't want to add to the confusion in shaft alley.

"Conn, the flooding has stopped," the EOOW went on. "I've just ordered another damage control team into shaft alley to complete make-shift repairs to the seals with emergency packing – but it's going to take five minutes. They need to remove the guards around the shaft and access the seals and emergency packing. Once the emergency repairs are completed, we can slowly depressurize the boot and start getting the main engines back on line."

"Maneuvering we don't have five minutes!" Richard Wickham's tone was edged with frantic desperation.

Maneuvering did not reply. Wickham tossed the handset microphone aside in frustration and strode to the diving control station. The planesman had the yoke control in his hands, his grip so tight his knuckles were white. He was holding the bow up at a twenty-degree angle, yet even with the ship's massive diving planes deployed, the boat was still sinking by the stern. Superstructure items creaked and popped, setting every man's nerves on edge. A sudden *'crack'* of noise sounded like a gunshot in the crushing tension.

"Passing four-hundred and fifty feet…" COB's tone became funereal. Wickham stole a glance at his wristwatch. The second hand seemed to be dragging.

"Chief of the Watch, conduct a two second emergency blow of the after main ballast tanks," the XO ordered. It was an order borne out of desperation – an attempt to arrest the submarine's descent without going to the surface and being counter-detected.

"Aye, sir," the COW repeated. "Conducting a two-second emergency blow of the after main ballast tanks." Before he carried out the order the COW reached for the 1MC. "The ship will be conducting a two-second emergency blow of the after main ballast tanks."

The Chief of the Watch reached up above his panel and felt for a large lever. As he shut the valve, a howl of hissing air sounded throughout the vessel.

In the stern engineering spaces, the damage control party was working with the frenzy of men possessed, each of them acutely aware of the rising peril. Slaving with hammers and wooden blocks and an array of machinist tools they tightened down the damaged seals, their fingers worn to broken mush, their hands covered in blood and grimy oil, near-blinded by stinging salt-water spray until there was no more they could do. Water was still hissing through the fractured seals, but at a rate the drain pumps could manage.

The JA command circuit above the conn squawked to life. Richard Wickham lunged for the handset.

"Conn, maneuvering. Emergency repairs are in place! The seals have a controlled leak rate and the drain pump is keeping up. We have recovered the engine room. We're ready to answer all bells. Recommend limiting propulsion to a two-third bell," the Engineering Officer of the Watch declared.

Richard Wickham glanced at his wristwatch. The emergency repairs had taken less than four minutes. He felt an enormous rush of gratitude and fierce pride for the men who had risked their lives. "Very well, maneuvering," he choked on his relief, then spun on his heel.

"Helm, all ahead two-thirds, make your depth one-fifty feet, limit your angle, right five-degrees, rudder steady, course zero-nine-zero."

"Aye, sir!" a wave of relief swept around the Control room and the Chief of the Boat repeated and passed along the orders.

The planesman already held the boat at a twenty-degree up angle, but now, as the submarine's engines re-started and propulsion was restored, *OKC* had speed to drive her through the water and help her ascend. Slowly – agonizingly slowly – the boat began to move forward. Still she descended, passing through five hundred feet before the ship's forward momentum built.

"Positive depth rate. Rising. Four-seventy-five feet and positive depth rate," COB's voice was almost reckless with relief. "Four-five-zero feet…"

Richard Wickham stole a moment to bow his head, draw a deep relieved breath, and offer a silent prayer of thanks to his god. Then he seemed to come alive with a fresh rush of energy. They were back in the fight, but now the struggle was to escape and survive.

"FCC, I need an update. Tell me what the hell is happening on the surface."

"The four destroyers, Master Thirty-Five, Thirty-Six, Thirty-Seven and Thirty-Eight that launched their attack on us are all eight thousand yards to the northwest. Two enemy helos still operating. The closest one is to the southeast of the destroyers but still seven thousand yards away. The helos are still dipping. I don't know what the hell they're hunting, but they're real determined," the ships' Engineer, acting in the capacity of the FCC, gave Wickham a succinct tactical summary.

"What about the two remaining destroyers?"

"Master Thirty-Nine and Master Forty are four thousand yards to the east, bearing zero-nine-four," the Engineer said. "I think they're collecting survivors from the sinking ships. Both destroyers are making random slow-speed course changes, moving at around five knots."

Richard Wickham could picture the scene; in his mind's eye he could see the two Chinese destroyers drifting amongst the debris, searching for injured men in the water.

"FCC, I want to know the second either of those two destroyers pick up speed and settles on a new heading. And keep an eye on those four destroyers to the northwest. If they begin to move closer to our position, I want to know about it immediately."

Wickham snatched for the JA command circuit and re-connected to maneuvering. A desperate plan was forming in his mind; a sliver of hope that the boat could escape the Chinese net and limp to safety.

"Engineering Officer of the Watch, keep the drain pumps going until I order otherwise. There's going to come a time in the not-too-distant future that you're going to need to shut them down so we can escape the enemy. So standby."

"Maneuvering, aye."

There was nothing else Richard Wickham could do. "Weps, you have the conn. I'm going to the wardroom to check on Captain Coe. I'll brief the Control room when I get back."

*

There were a dozen injured crewmen slumped in the narrow passageway outside the officer's wardroom with more injured men waiting in the crew's mess. Many of the wounded were nursing broken bones and deep cuts. Wickham recognized two of the men from the damage control party he had led to the water-tight door. He stopped to talk to the men briefly and to thank the injured for their dedication and sacrifice, then gingerly stepped past the awkward tangle of limbs and stood in the threshold to the wardroom.

For a gut-swooping moment of icy-cold dread, he thought Chris Coe was dead. The ship's Captain was stretched out on the wardroom table, unmoving. His face was ashen, his features so haggard as to be almost unrecognizable. The top of his head was swathed in a thick roll of bandages and there was more strapping on one of his lower legs. The floor around the tabletop was strewn with blood-soaked gauze.

As Wickham drew closer, Chris Coe's eyes flickered open, vague and unfocussed. The XO felt an overwhelming sense of relief.

"I'm not dead yet, XO," Coe croaked through dry, parched lips.

"Relieved to hear it, sir," Wickham smiled, despite himself.

"We're in a bad way?"

"Yes, sir," The XO summed up the boat's perilous situation in just a few terse sentences.

Coe grunted. His breath rattled in his throat and he closed his eyes again. For a moment Wickham thought the Captain had slipped into the dark void of unconsciousness, but then Coe's head turned and his eyes were suddenly bright and sharp.

"Do you remember that damned foolhardy maneuver we tried in the simulator about six months ago, XO? The one with the emergency turn…?"

"Yes, sir," Wickham said, suddenly frowning. "I do…"

"It might be time," Coe grimaced as searing pain shot up his leg. He gasped and clenched his teeth until the pain subsided. "It might be time to test it out in a real combat situation…"

Wickham blanched. "Sir, it was just a simulation…"

Coe's hand slid from his side and seized the XO's arm. New strength and conviction came into the Captain's voice. *"You can do it, XO. The men trust you. And I trust you."* The powerful moment seemed to drain the last reserves of Chris Coe's energy. He slumped back against the table and the tension melted from his body. His eyes closed and unconsciousness wrapped itself around him like a dark blanket.

"Is…is he…?" Wickham turned to the ship's independent duty corpsman. His voice went very quiet.

"He's unconscious," the man peeled off a pair of blood-smeared rubber surgical gloves and dropped them on the deck. He was a short, stocky man of Iranian descent with dark olive skin and black curly hair; a highly-trained paramedic-level E6. "He might have a skull fracture, although I can't be sure at this stage. He definitely has a severe concussion, as well as some deep lacerations on his leg. I've given him Penicillin against infection and done all I can to dress his head wound."

"Is his condition life-threatening?"

"Probably not," the Doc shook his head. He was a humorless man who took his work seriously. "But he's going to be out of action for several days at least."

"Is there anything else you can do?"

"Not until we return to port."

The handset for the JA Command Circuit buzzed. The Doc reached under the table, listened for a moment and then hung up, his expression unreadable. "XO, you're needed back in Control. Apparently, it's urgent."

*

"What have you got?" Richard Wickham demanded as he passed through Control and pushed his way into the cramped confines of the sonar shack.

The Sonar Supervisor pointed at the bank of monitors, their screens glowing in the soft blue light that filled the room.

"Master Thirty-Nine and Master Forty are on the move," the Supervisor explained. "They're headed west, and now bear zero-three-zero to the northeast of us and are making about eight knots."

"That means there are no more Chinese survivors," Wickham deduced. "The destroyers will be heading back to the Chinese mainland, dangerously overloaded with hundreds of injured men. That's why they're moving so slowly."

It made sense. The Sonar Supervisor could put forward no alternative hypothesis.

"What about the rest of the Chinese destroyers?"

"Master Thirty-Five and Master Thirty-Eight have turned southwest. Current bearing is two-nine-zero, moving further away. Master Thirty-Six and Thirty-Seven seem to have called off the search for us and are heading south, probably intending to intercept the destroyers carrying their survivors to escort them to safety."

Richard Wickham grunted. He folded his arms and stared thoughtfully at the displays but his mind was elsewhere, enmeshed in a series of complex calculations based on the premise of a reckless gamble.

He squared his shoulders and strode aft to the conn. It was time to roll the dice one last time.

"Sonar, conn. Range to Masters Thirty-Nine and Forty?"

"Conn, sonar. Range to Master Thirty-Nine is three thousand yards, bearing zero-three-four, speed eight knots. Master Forty is directly astern of her."

"Sonar, aye," the XO acknowledged. "Helm right ten-degree rudder. Steady course one-five-zero."

"Right ten-degree rudder steady course one-five-zero. Sir, my rudder is right ten."

"Very well, helm."

"Passing course one-four-zero to the right…ten-degrees from ordered course… Now steady on course one-five-zero, sir."

Finally, Richard Wickham stole a moment and quickly addressed the Control room. "Attention Control. There are two Chinese destroyers to our northeast. They have just picked up the last of the Chinese survivors of the ships we attacked, and they are now steaming west and will pass close to us to the north. We are to the southeast of them. It is my intention to wait until the two enemy ships approach us, and as they CPA (closest point of approach) us to the north, we will quickly come all the way around to the west and tuck in under them on a westerly course and transit under their hulls right behind them. Once we are past the actively searching Chinese destroyers coming down from the northwest, we will fade away and evade to the north. Are there any questions? Any comments?"

No one spoke, but Richard Wickham could see the stunned, disbelieving expressions on their faces. He knew what they were thinking. *"Are you crazy?"*

"Very well," the XO spoke across the shocked silence. "COB, pass on the phones for all stations to man battle stations!"

"Aye, sir."

Wickham snatched for the phones above his head and called maneuvering. "Engineering Officer of the Watch, secure all damage control efforts. Secure the pumps now!"

"Maneuvering, eye. Securing all DC efforts."

"COB, rig ship for ultra-quiet!" It wasn't technically possible because the submarine was making errant noise through the leaking seals and the constantly running pumps. But the message was still important.

The ship is in imminent danger. Remain as quiet as possible!

"Aye, sir!"

Oklahoma City was moving off the approaching destroyers track and slightly opening the distance between herself and the two overloaded Chinese destroyers, like a huge eighteen-wheel semi-trailer truck needing to swing wide across the highway in order to prepare for an upcoming hairpin turn. As the orders were echoed around Control and the submarine cut through the ocean, Richard Wickham had one last opportunity to change his mind before he committed himself. The XO clenched his fists, standing his ground until the moment passed, then thrust out his jaw with grim determination. There was only one desperate hope of escape and now *OKC* was compelled, it was his duty to see it through.

"Diving officer, make your depth one-two-zero feet." The change of depth was not a random number Wickham had plucked from the ether. It was, in fact, a careful calculation; a guestimation of the Chinese destroyer's draft now that she was overloaded with hundreds of injured Chinese sailors, and his own knowledge of *OKCs* dimensions. A 688 submarine measured fifty feet from the keel to the top of the sail. Wickham guessed the Chinese destroyer, heavily overloaded, would be drawing around forty feet. That gave him a margin of thirty feet – if his estimations were right…

Oklahoma City reached a depth of one-two-zero feet and leveled off, still closing on the Chinese Type 052C *Luyang II*-class destroyers. The distance between the two closed quickly until the range was less than a thousand yards. The Chinese ship's engines were laboring under the enormous load she was carrying. The Control room went eerily quiet as each man held his breath, listing to the straining sound of the enemy ship through the submarine's hull. Then a warning from the sonar shack cut through the thick tension.

"Conn, sonar! Master Thirty-Six and Thirty-Seven have changed course and are accelerating. Bearing now two-eight-one and closing on us, making eighteen knots. Range four thousand yards."

Richard Wickham froze, and a lump of dread lodged in his chest.

Had the Chinese destroyers somehow detected them and were now closing for the kill… or were they merely rendezvousing with the two overloaded destroyers, perhaps to offload some of the injured?

His mind leaped to another set of complex calculations. Master Thirty-Six and Thirty-Seven would be on top of *OKC* in six and a half minutes. The two overloaded Chinese destroyers approaching from the northeast would reach his position in less than four minutes.

The slightest mistake now would be disastrous.

Wickham counted down the seconds, his eyes on the overhead displays, watching the two Chinese surface groups converging on his location. The two overloaded destroyers passed a few hundred yards to the north of the submarine, the enemy ships screws churning through the water and leaving a wake of turbulence.

Every man in Control lifted their eyes to the overhead. There was less than thirty feet of clearance between the passing hull of the destroyer and the top of *Oklahoma City's* sail. The submarine began to wallow, buffeted by the maelstrom of water that washed around it.

"COB, vent the after main ballast tank group."

"Aye, sir! Venting the after group of ballast tanks." That was important. *Oklahoma City's* after main ballast tanks needed to be completely filled with water for fine depth control before he gave the next sequence of orders.

"Helm! Left fifteen-degree rudder. All ahead standard. Maneuvering, cavitate!"

The helmsman pressed a button on the engine order telegraph three times which buzzed in maneuvering where the throttleman rapidly opened the ship's main turbine throttles.

The submarine's speed rose sharply. Wickham waited a few seconds and then gave his next order. "Helm increase your rudder to left full."

The orders were repeated with the same urgency they were issued, and the helmsman steered the submarine hard to the left. He was sweating under the strain as was the planesman sitting beside him. Both men fixated on the readouts in front of them, aware that any error could have fatal consequences.

"Passing course zero-nine-zero to the left. No ordered course. My rudder is left full!"

"Very well, helm."

"Passing course north to the left. No ordered course. My rudder is left full…"

Richard Wickham counted to twenty in his head, drew a last deep breath, and suddenly barked, "Helm, shift your rudder! Steady course two-seven-zero!"

"Aye, sir! My rudder is shifted to right full, steadying course two-seven-zero, all ahead two thirds!"

Oklahoma City responded as if the ship was a living thing that also sensed the high-stakes game being played out. She turned hard, her huge rudder cutting cleanly through the ocean, her planes holding her rigidly at one-two-zero feet as she cornered like a thoroughbred and turned directly astern and beneath the second Chinese destroyer; Master Forty.

"Christ!" the blasphemy was wrenched from the Diving Officer's throat at the sheer audacious brilliance of the maneuver. He stared at his boards for long, stunned seconds and then breathed, "Jesus. You've done it, Mister Wickham. We're beneath and directly astern of the trailing Chinese destroyer, hidden in her baffles. Our noise is being completely masked from the enemy by their own engine noise and wash."

"Helm, ahead two-thirds. Have maneuvering make turns for eight knots!" Wickham ordered the submarine's speed reduced to match the speed of the destroyer above them. The XO couldn't take even a moment to reflect on the success of the maneuver; *OKC* was still not out of danger. He strode forward and burst into the sonar shack.

"Keep an eye on Master Forty," Wickham demanded. "I want to know the instant there is even a hint of aspect change or any sign of her slowing or accelerating. Understand?"

"Aye, sir!" It wouldn't be that simple. With the *OKC* directly behind the Chinese destroyer and only just below the surface, the submarine's sonar displays would be rendered almost useless due to the 'near field effect' – caused by sounds coming from so close to the boat that the hydrophones would have difficulty getting a good bearing.

Wickham returned to the Control room and stepped up to the conn. "Raising the Number Two scope!" he announced.

The Diving Officer of the Watch responded. "Raising Number Two scope. Depth one-two-zero feet, speed eight knots, aye, sir."

This was a risky maneuver, but the American fast-attack boat crews trained on this procedure and indeed each submarine had a code phrase for the evolution in case the surface vessel they were monitoring suddenly changed course. The code phrase would activate an immediate dive to one hundred and fifty feet, the scope would be quickly lowered, and two-thirds speed rung up – all automatically if the alert phrase was uttered. It was a tactic and capability very few outside the submarine force were aware of, and one that submariners kept a closely-guarded secret.

The tension ratcheted up again inside the Control room as the ship's periscope rose into the ocean. Richard Wickham met the scope as it slid up from its well and pressed his left eye to the viewer. The sea below the surface was a froth of white churning water. Two hundred yards ahead he noticed the submerged stern and screws of the Chinese destroyer, Master Forty. Wickham watched the wake being tossed by her screws and saw the ship's hull low in the water. He rotated the left handle of the scope which controlled elevation. The scope assistant standing beside the XO called out, "Positive elevation..." which meant that the images of the Chinese destroyer being displayed on the Control room's television screens were *above them*. It was critical information. If the elevation on the scope's handle became negative it meant the submarine, with its scope extended, was too shallow and she would be on a submerged collision course with the destroyer.

Raising the scope was a precarious and risk-filled evolution – but critical to Wickham's plan. Now he was certain that *Oklahoma City* was indeed below the hull of the Chinese destroyer and there was no longer a risk of submerged collision, the next phase was to match speeds. He steadied the scope on one of the destroyer's screws and gauged the range for several seconds. He sensed *OKC* was closing the distance...

"Maneuvering down one turn!"

The order was repeated and *OKC* slowed until her speed was perfectly matched to the enemy vessel.

Finally, Wickham steadied on the center of the destroyer's screws to have the FCC mark the bearing. "Bearing to Master

Forty's screws... Bearing mark!" He thumbed the scope button that sent the bearing to Fire Control.

"Bearing two-seven-three!" The FCC called out.

"Helm," Wickham reacted quickly. "Steer course two-seven-three."

"Aye, sir! Making my course two-seven-three."

It was done. *OKC* was at a safe depth, her speed was perfectly matched to the destroyer above them, and they were steering the enemy ship's exact course. Wickham released a deep breath of air he hadn't realized had been jammed in his throat. His hands were trembling. "Down scope!"

For twenty-five more taut and nerve-racking minutes, the *Oklahoma City* followed the two overburdened Chinese destroyers, clinging to their wake and lost in the churning maelstrom of their baffles. Richard Wickham took a long look around the Control room. Order throughout the ship had been restored. The ships pumps were silent, and the boat had continued to take on water, but not enough to yet be a problem. Lighting had been restored and the sound-powered phones were working again.

"Chief of the Boat, ahead one third," Richard Wickham ordered.

"Ahead one third, aye," COB repeated the command.

Gradually *OKC* slowed, losing forward momentum. "Diving Officer of the Watch, use a ten-degree down angle. Make your depth three-four-zero feet."

The submarine drifted down, silent, and unheard, until it reached a depth of three hundred and forty feet and then hung suspended in the ocean by neutral buoyancy.

Wickham let the boat drift for a further fifteen minutes at low speed until the water being shipped aboard from the slow-leaking seals began to drag the boat's stern, altering her trim. The Chinese warships had continued west, still making for the mainland, and were fourth thousand yards away, the distance increasing with every minute.

Wickham reached for the phones overhead. "Maneuvering, this is the XO. You can re-start the drain pumps in the engine room."

"Maneuvering, aye."

Richard Wickham hung up the phone and turned to the COB, but in reality, he was addressing every man in Control. "COB, all ahead two thirds," the XO tried to keep his voice matter-of-fact, but there was a sudden unmistakable edge of satisfaction and triumph in his tone. "Make your course due north. We're going home."

Epilogue:

The wound on the Captain's leg had begun to heal but the traces of ordeal in Chris Coe's haggard face remained. His skin was pale, his jaw unshaven, and his eyes were sunk deep into their sockets and rimmed with dark smudge-like bruises. His head was still swathed in bandages as he sat propped up in his stateroom bunk.

"COB told me you executed the simulator plan to get the boat to safety," Chris Coe was his usual irascible and impatient self, but he was also somehow changed. "And that you did so flawlessly." Richard Wickham saw it in the man's eyes; dark shadows moving with some secret emotion that could have been fear, or anger, or perhaps contrition. "That was a fine piece of leadership."

"Thank you, sir," Wickham was inordinately pleased with the praise.

"Where are we?"

"The East China Sea," Wickham explained, "bound for Yokosuka." It had been seventy-two hours since the attack on the Chinese flotilla and in that time the submarine had slowly, but steadily, continued steering north. "We've been ordered to Fleet Activities for urgent repairs."

"What about the Qingdao convoy?" Coe suddenly sat upright in the bunk and winced from the effort.

"The Chinese ships never left port," Richard Wickham shrugged his shoulders. "Intel still doesn't know if the whole story was a Chinese counter-intelligence operation to distract us from the imminent invasion fleet sailing into the Taiwan Strait, or whether the Chinese changed plans and shipped the arms across the country to Pakistan. Either way, they drew two of our *Virginia*-class boats out of combat operations for several days – with nothing to show for their effort."

Chris Coe grunted. He seemed to hesitate for a moment and then he shaped his features into a stern expression. "Everything you have done to save the ship is negated by your disobedience of orders, XO," Coe's voice rasped. "I gave you a direct order to keep that water-tight door sealed until the boat reached safety. You disobeyed my instruction."

"Yes," Richard Wickham said.

"Do you have anything to say in your defense?"

"*Sir, your orders were a guide to my actions. But as the Executive Officer of a US attack submarine my decisions are governed by my instincts,*" Richard Wickham threw Chris Coe's own words back at him. "A well-respected submarine commander taught me that lesson, and when I was forced to take action, I remembered his words."

Coe flinched as if he had been slapped in the face, and then his eyes turned foxy and a hint of his old sea-dog personality shone through. Richard Wickham recognized the look hidden in his commanding officer's eyes at last. It hadn't been fear, or even contrition…

It was respect.

"Very well, Mister Wickham," Chris Coe nodded his head to acknowledge he had been cleverly bested. "Carry on…"

Facebook: https://www.facebook.com/NickRyanWW3
Website: https://www.worldwar3timeline.com

Acknowledgements:

The greatest thrill of writing, for me, is the opportunity to research the subject matter and to work with military, political and historical experts from around the world. I had a lot of help researching this book from the following groups and people. I am forever grateful for their willing enthusiasm and cooperation.

Any remaining technical errors are mine.

Jill Blasy:

Jill has the editorial eye of an eagle! I trust Jill to read every manuscript, picking up typographical errors, missing commas, and for her general 'sense' of the book. Jill has been a great friend and a valuable part of my team for several years.

Jan Wade:

Jan is my Personal Assistant and an indispensable part of my team. She is a thoughtful, thorough, professional and persistent pleasure to work with. Chances are, if you're reading this book, it's due to Jan's engaging marketing and promotional efforts.

Members of the US Submarine Service

The US Submarine service remains very much the 'Silent Service'. For operational security of follow-on generations, submariners of all ranks do their best not to share any specifics of actual past or on-going operations. This unwritten rule applies to the highest-ranking officers right down to the young cook or torpedoman who might only serve a few years; they all live to the same commitment.

While writing this book I had a tremendous amount of help from two retired high-ranking US Naval Officers who both wish to remain anonymous.

I respect their decision.

I'm endlessly grateful for the technical and tactical help these retired SSN Commanders gave me. Without their patient checking and re-checking of the manuscript, this book could never have happened. This story portrays the operational tempos and engagement situations of modern submarine warfare as authentically and accurately as fiction allows.

Printed in Great Britain
by Amazon